WINDRAIL

THE SECRET MEETING PLACE

By

Andrew F. Maksymchuk

With

Evan D. Maksymchuk & Rylan Maksymchuk

SONG LYRICS IN THIS BOOK

Land Of The Maple Tree
Words and Music by Tom Charles Connors and Arthur H. Hawes
Copyright (c) 1969 Crown Vetch Music
Copyright Renewed

The Flyin' C.P.R.
Words and Music by Tom Charles Connors
Copyright (c) 1969 Crown Vetch Music
Copyright Renewed

Canada Day, Up Canada Way
Words and Music by Tom Charles Connors
Copyright (c) 1993 Crown Vetch Music

Confederation Bridge
Words and Music by Tom Charles Connors
Copyright (c) 1999 Crown Vetch Music

Sudbury Saturday Night
Words and Music by Tom Charles Connors
Copyright (c) 1969 Crown Vetch Music
Copyright Renewed

<u>Initial critique and computer assistance from:</u>
Lesa Maksymchuk,
Ottawa, Ontario

<u>Edited by:</u>
Kay Griffiths, Comox, BC

<u>Front Cover Photo by:</u>
Christine Bertoli, Sudbury, Ontario

Author with Illustrators Evan &
Rylan Maksymchuk, Sudbury,
Ontario, at Skinners Pond, PEI

Illustrator T.L. "Skippy" Drew (right) with his masterpiece of two
Wannabee Canadian animals in Wodonga, Victoria, Australia.

DEDICATION

To the people of Ukraine, bravely fighting for their country, freedom and a wonderful way of life.

Stompin' Tom experienced the pleasures of Ukrainian cultural hospitality as he rode his thumb across the Canadian Prairies. He paid tribute to those hosts and hostesses through the lyrics and tempo of their favourite dance style with...

Zakuska Polka.

ABOUT THE BOOK

The book you are about to read, aimed at youngsters, is primarily a work of fiction. It does, however, contain many educational facts of Canadiana that may surprise even the most learned of all ages.

Visitors and those planning to become permanent residents will probably find it very informative.

The wonders of our country, from sea to sea to sea, and the animals and people therein that call it home, never cease to amaze.

AFM
oppmaks@gmail.com

TABLE OF CONTENTS

Chapter One   The Sleepover   1
Chapter Two   Stompin' Tom Connors   9
Chapter Three   Kildare Capes   19
Chapter Four   The Sixth Sense   27
Chapter Five   North Cape   32
Chapter Six   Maples and Smudging   36
Chapter Seven   Terrifying Screams   42
Chapter Eight   Noisy Nick   52
Chapter Nine   Evil Monsters   57
Chapter Ten   Sasha Sasquatch   63
Chapter Eleven   Olga Ogopogo   75
Chapter Twelve   Bazil The Black-Tailed Prairie Dog   90
Chapter Thirteen   Red River Renée, B.Eng.   117
Chapter Fourteen   Uninvited Human-Eaters   142
Chapter Fifteen   Welcomed Visitors   153
Chapter Sixteen   Canada's Big Five   164
Chapter Seventeen   Waiting For Their Hero   169
Chapter Eighteen   The Disappearing Statue   174
Acknowledgements   179

CHAPTER ONE

THE SLEEPOVER

The day after Grandma and Grandpa returned home from a trip to Africa, two excited children burst in through their front door. It was granddaughter Emma and grandson Traedan, eager and excited to hear about their grandparents' adventures, especially those on safari in Kenya's Serengeti.

After the grandkids had been calmed and seated, each grandparent told of some of the things they had seen and done on their holiday. Then, when the conversation got around to unique animals, Grandpa said, "During our safari we were lucky enough to observe all of Africa's Big Five animals, a must-see for tourists."

"Which animals are they, Grandpa?" asked Traedan.

"The elephant, lion, rhinoceros, Cape buffalo, and leopard," he replied. "The leopard was the most difficult for us to find because they're nocturnal. It was our good fortune that Grandma noticed one asleep on a tree branch in mid-afternoon," he said, as Grandma joyfully showed the children a picture she had taken of the awaking spotted cat.

"Not all of them are *that* big," said Emma. "Why are they all called Big Five?"

Africa's Big Five Animals

"That title was given to them by big game trophy hunters who found them to be Africa's most difficult animals to hunt on foot," explained Grandpa. "When hunting greatly reduced their numbers, licences to hunt them became very expensive and today only a few are issued for national parks like the Serengeti. A safari is mainly for picture-taking and sight-seeing nowadays, but poachers still hunt them illegally. The elephants are killed for their ivory tusks to make jewellery and ornaments, the rhinoceros for their horns which some people incorrectly believe to have medicinal value, and the leopards and lions for their skins. The rhinos are now seriously endangered."

"Does Canada have a Big Five animal list, Grandpa?" questioned Traedan.

"Canada tried to make a list several years ago, but it never became official," he responded, "And it certainly didn't have anything to do with sport hunting. The list I'm referring to was supposed to identify animals that tourists from around the world would most wish to see, watch, photograph or video in their natural habitat.

"I can tell you a story about the animals that almost became the first official ones on Canada's Big Five list. But it's a long one," Grandpa said, "So if you wish to hear it, you had better call your parents and ask if you can stay for dinner and a sleepover."

The children were elated!

With permission from their parents to stay overnight, it wasn't long after the evening meal before Traedan and Emma were in their pyjamas and curled up on the comfortable couch, anxiously waiting for Grandpa to begin his story.

Grandma brought out hot cups of cocoa and a huge bowl of Ukrainian deep-fried cookies called *khrustyky* (hroo-steh-key) for everyone to enjoy. Because of their shape, Grandpa called the sweet pastry treats "bow ties" while Grandma referred to them as "angel wings."

"They look like pig ears to me!" mumbled Traedan with a mouthful as he gleefully chewed a huge bite.

Khrustyky

Grandma was the last to join the group. She had heard the tale before, but with her iPad in hand, she would quietly play her favourite game of solitaire while being available to Google any topics or questions that might arise.

When everyone was settled and munching on their treats, Grandpa said, "Some of the world's most spectacular creatures, including about 200 different species of mammals, call Canada their home. Some of them can't be found anywhere else in the world. For the same reasons that your Grandma and I travelled to Africa, people from other countries come here to satisfy their interest and curiosity in our unusual, extraordinary and remarkable animals still living free in their natural territory.

"Tourism is great for our economy but it is also our duty to protect our animals, learn to coexist with them and provide them with as natural an environment as possible so they will not become extinct. Too many are already on the Endangered or At Risk lists from being over-trapped and over-hunted. Others have decreased in number from human mismanagement and misuse of lands, forests and oceans in the greedy reaping of the world's natural resources. We must learn and work to make room for everyone."

Then Grandpa began, "Once upon a time...," and the kids broke into laughter.

"You always start your stories that way!" Traedan and Emma chimed in together.

"Okay," chuckled Grandpa, "Let's try it this way," and he began again.

"Several years ago, Canada decided to identify the top five wild animals most probably on tourists' must-see lists. So the people formed a government committee and after many months of study and meetings, the names of the five types of animals selected were presented to the Prime Minister. But before the list became official, it had leaked out to the public. And although it was impressive, it was also controversial."

"The top five animals selected by the committee were:

Grizzly Bear   Moose   Polar Bear

Wolf   Bison (also called Buffalo)

"For reasons unknown," continued Grandpa, "only land mammals and a polar bear had been suggested for the five positions.

"Complaints began to pour into the Prime Minister's office at the Parliament Buildings in Ottawa, Ontario, Canada's capital city. Some came from people but most were from the animals themselves."

"'With Canada describing itself as a country from sea to sea to sea, why weren't the marine mammals living in and beside the waters along the Pacific, Atlantic and Arctic Ocean coasts considered?' bubbled a beluga whale from Mackenzie Bay on the northern Yukon Territory shore. 'We're very Canadian. We don't have a dorsal fin so we can swim under the ice in shallow northern waters and are white as snow. We need more attention since we *are* on the Endangered list!'"

Beluga Whale

"A similar complaint was echoed by a blue whale from the Gulf of St. Lawrence. Already on the At Risk list, it added, 'The wood bison may deserve to be selected. They're the largest land animal in North America and have their head image on the cap badge of the Royal Canadian Mounted Police, but we're the largest animals on earth!'"

Blue Whale

RCMP Cap Badge

"The caribou wondered why *they* weren't picked since their image has been on the Canadian 25 cent coin – called a quarter – for over eighty years,

Caribou (also called Reindeer)

Quarter (Twenty-five cents - 25¢)

'and we have to keep fit and ready to pull Santa's sleigh around the world on Christmas Eve, too!' they reasoned."

"Then the birds chirped in, 'Not one feather-covered Canadian was considered even though the Canada goose was named after our nation and has a huge statue in Wawa, Ontario. And an image of a loon is on our one dollar coin nicknamed a loonie!,' they squawked."

Canada Goose Statue
Wawa, Ontario

Loonie
(One Dollar)

Common Loon

Loonie Statue, Echo Bay, Ontario
Coin Designed by Robert-Ralph Carmichael

"With so many complaints being received," said Grandpa, "there apparently was only one thing left to do. The Prime Minister sent for the one person he believed would be able to settle the matter to everyone's satisfaction.

"The way the story was told to me," continued Grandpa, "the person the Prime Minister had in mind was extremely patriotic and an Officer of the

Order of Canada, the highest award in Canada's honours system.

"By way of an appointment, any Canadian citizen having made a difference and enriched the lives of others, may be recognized for their extraordinary contributions to our country. Expressed in songs by the artistic person in this instance, was the overall style he saw in the lives of Canadians within the magnificent landscape of their homeland.

"He had hitchhiked to every corner of our country, written and sung about everything Canadian, was honest, humble, friendly, and kind to all. He was a folk and country song troubadour, won seven Juno Awards, received three Honorary Doctorate degrees and was inducted into Canada's Walk of Fame.

"He has also been referred to as Canada's best unofficial ambassador to people around the world. Above all, he seemed to have a special knack of being able to communicate and get along with all living creatures, including many of the world's most spectacular animals that call Canada home.

"The man I'm speaking of is the most Canadian of Canadian musicians. None other than...**STOMPIN' TOM CONNORS.**"

CHAPTER TWO

STOMPIN' TOM CONNORS

Order of Canada Medal

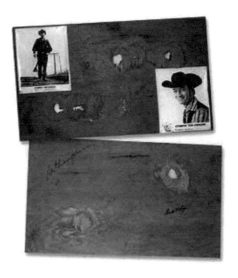

Dr.Thomas Charles Connors,
O.C., LL.D., Litt.D.
(aka Stompin' Tom)

Stompin' Boards

D oes anyone in this room know who Stompin' Tom is?" Grandpa teasingly asked.

"Yes!" Emma cried out, leaping off the couch and stamping her feet.

"And *The Hockey Song* is always played at our hockey games!" added Traedan, as he started singing Stompin' Tom's familiar song so loudly it practically forced his sister to join him in a duet. "He stomps his foot and sings about Canada."

Taking advantage of the opportunity, Grandpa grabbed his nearby guitar and began to play and sing along with his grandchildren. Even Grandma joined in on time to create a quartet as the third and final verse, about the third and final period, brought the song to a hilarious end.

"I think everyone in Canada knows the words to that famous tune!" an out-of-breath Grandma exclaimed. "It's so popular it has almost become a part of our national winter sport itself. I wonder if Stompin' Tom has written a song about lacrosse, our national summer sport, as well," she puffed to no one in particular.

When everyone had finally settled down from their impromptu musical outburst, Grandpa set his guitar aside and continued his story.

"Some people call this tale legendary and others call it a myth, but this is the way it was told to me and each and every one who hears it can be their own judge." Grandpa then went on to say, "Stompin' Tom was probably hard at work, composing yet another song about Canada to add to the hundreds he had already written, when he apparently received a call from the Prime

Minister. His belief in service to his country was far too strong for him to refuse, so I'm sure he would have unhesitatingly agreed to the request for assistance. It has been said that his only stipulation was that he be allowed to proceed without interference and with the utmost secrecy in order to protect all animals and humans from one another. Since no one today is aware of many of the details, the Prime Minister must have agreed to the code of secrecy.

"What is true is that Stompin' Tom was born in Saint John, New Brunswick but raised by a foster family in Skinners Pond, Prince Edward Island – or PEI as everyone calls Canada's smallest province. PEI is also known as the Birthplace of Canada for hosting the first Confederation meeting of British colonies in 1864 in what is now Canada, at its capital city of Charlottetown. That gathering led to the formation of a new country called Canada three years later.

"Stompin' Tom probably reasoned that if a new country could be borne out of a meeting, the best way to resolve the Big Five situation would be to have the animals make the decisions for themselves. That meant, of course, he would have to find a place for the animals to meet and a way of communicating with them.

"Even though he had zigzagged across Canada many times by hitchhiking and hopping freight trains, Stompin' Tom was most familiar with PEI, his adopted province, and hoped he could find a suitable location somewhere between the tips of its crescent shape. The secret meeting place would have to be accessible by land, air and sea, and provide enough space for animals classed as land mammals, marine mammals, reptiles, birds, and amphibians to gather. It would be like a boat-less and one-animal-of-each-kind-only Noah's Ark. For everyone's safety, it would also have to be very secluded.

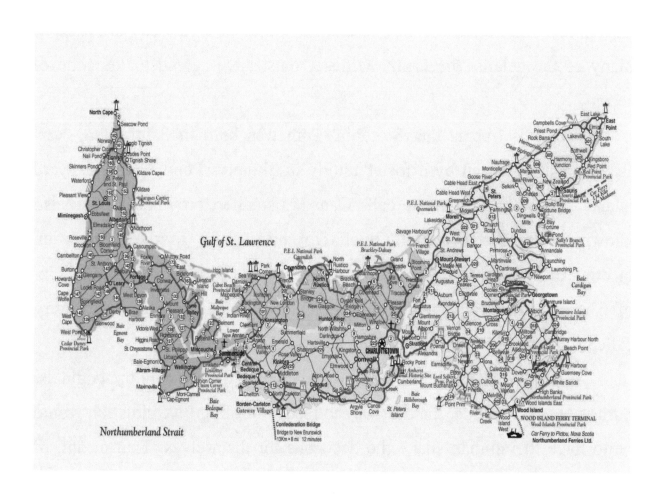

Prince Edward Island (PEI)

"PEI is the most densely populated of all provinces, but its western one-third, called Prince County, is the more sparsely settled and provides kilometres of secluded beaches, high rugged capes, large wooded areas and clear open spaces. Included within the boundaries of that county are the traditional lands of the Lennox Island Mi'kmaq (Micmac) First Nation."

Lennox Island First Nation Logo

Grandpa went on to say, "The Mi'kmaq were the first known humans to inhabit the land of Canada's Atlantic provinces, arriving over ten thousand years ago. Those that chose PEI as their home referred to the island as Abegweit (*Epekwitk*) which means 'cradle on the waves.' Sadly, that beautiful name disappeared with several possession and name changes by France and England, Canada's feuding Mother Countries. Prince Edward Island finally became known what it is today when it was ceded to England and named after a prince of Great Britain who had never even set foot on its soil. Apparently the Mi'kmaq weren't consulted on any of the name changes.

"The Mi'kmaq believe in living a simple life in harmony and with respect to all of nature and the animals on earth. Today, the community on Lennox Island is still steeped in culture and traditions that have been passed down through the ages. It is a lifestyle combining history, spiritual traditions, folklore and legends, including the guidance of *Glooscap* (klue-skopp), their legendary figure and cultural hero from the spirit world. The Mi'kmaq Chief, was the obvious person to ask for assistance.

A statue of Glooscap, over 12 metres tall,
at the Millbrook First Nation in Truro, Nova Scotia

"When approached," continued Grandpa, "the Mi'kmaq Chief took little time in consulting with, and arranging for, an Elder to help in the search for a suitable location to hold a meeting of the animals.

"The position of Elder is very important within the Mi'kmaq community.

It's a title that must be earned and has to do with actions and respect. Elders teach, are mentors, and encourage others to respect people for who they are without judging them.

"Since everything was done in utmost secrecy, any involvement of Stompin' Tom and his association with the Mi'kmaq people and various animals of Canada was never officially recorded," said Grandpa. "I can only pass on what I've heard and read over time through gossip, rumours, written history and friends in the know."

"A few days later at Lennox Island, the Mi'kmaq Chief introduced Stompin' Tom to Elder Mathilda as his choice of guides. In separate vehicles she led him to the shore of Cape Kildare just north of Jacques Cartier Provincial Park where the North Cape Coastal Drive Highway swings closest to the gulf and is sometimes level with the tips of the ocean waves on windy days.

"The site is historic. It is in the vicinity of the sailing ship landing of French navigator Jacques Cartier way back in 1534. Referring to it as 'Canada,' Cartier was the first European to explore the area, including the island of Abegweit (PEI), of what is now the Gulf of St. Lawrence, and claimed it all for France.

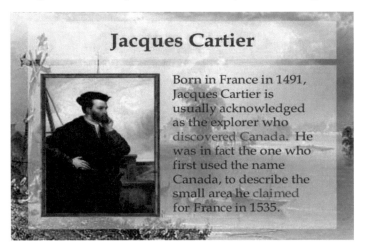

Jacques Cartier

Born in France in 1491, Jacques Cartier is usually acknowledged as the explorer who discovered Canada. He was in fact the one who first used the name Canada, to describe the small area he claimed for France in 1535.

Photo courtesy of Tourism, Alberton, PEI

15

"Cartier could hardly have known at the time, but the red-earth island would eventually become known as the Birthplace of Canada and then become part of Canada itself. It now seemed to have excellent possibilities in providing a good area for *The Secret Meeting Place.*

"Leg-clutching marram grass greeted the two searchers as they stepped from their vehicles onto an impromptu parking area used by beach-goers and Irish moss gatherers. On warm, sunny days the small beach area provides a quiet place for a few swimmers and sun-worshippers, but when the winds are blowing up a storm and rolling the ocean waters roughly to the shore, the parking area becomes a totally different scene. It quickly fills with pickup trucks – some towing horses on trailers – and instantly becomes a beehive of activity. In his song about gathering Irish moss, Stompin' Tom calls it 'one big hullaballoo' when he describes the higgledy-piggledy scene.

Horse and scoop gathering Irish Moss in PEI

"Using rakes and forks, people of all ages work among horses harnessed to scoops to take advantage of the bounty being offered by the sea.

"Called Irish moss, it is a special seaweed that has been ripped from ocean bottom rocks by wicked whirling waters, then brought close to shore by the waves for anyone to gather. The gift from the ocean depths doesn't come without its hazards, however, and tragic stories of drownings of humans and horses over the years still come to the minds of local families."

"What do they do with the Irish moss, Grandpa?" interrupted Emma.

"Well, I know that everyone in this room has eaten a lot of it," replied Grandpa.

"Yuck...I've never eaten any seaweed," said Traedan.

"I think we all have," laughed Grandma, looking up from her iPad. "After it's collected, Irish moss is dried and processed into what is called carrageenan and we use it to thicken, preserve, gel and stabilize many foods such as ice cream, yogurt, canned milk as well as many other foods, cosmetics, toothpaste, medicines and even beer," said Grandma, "But let's let Grandpa get back to his story and we can talk about that interesting topic at another time."

"As I was about to say," Grandpa continued, "Elder Mathilda and Stompin' Tom were standing at the lowest point of the Capes of Kildare. She explained to him that they would now have to walk an upward trail to where the red cliffs were at their highest and very difficult to scale from the edge of the waters below. The Elder went on to say that they would be passing through a rugged forest before reaching a huge open field abutting the coast. She said she believed Stompin' Tom would find it well suited for a secret place to gather. It was a longer walk than the unused overgrown path through the tangled woods from the highway, but much less physically challenging.

"And so the two set off along the edge of the shore, climbing with the capes towards their maximum height."

CHAPTER THREE

KILDARE CAPES

Elder Mathilda and Stompin' Tom found their hike along the top lip of Kildare Capes to be a greater challenge than expected," Grandpa told his small audience. "But according to them, the rustic conditions were even more ideally suited for the unique animal event."

He then went on to describe the capes so that his grandchildren would have a better picture in their mind during his story.

"The Capes of Kildare are tall rock cliffs of rugged red sandstone rising out of the sea," he said. "Only at low tide does a narrow ledge of water-polished rock and loose shale provide a slippery path for sure-footed and daring beachcombers. Over time, furious waves have carved inlets, arches, tunnels and short-depth caves into the vertical face of the snaking shoreline. Trapped sand covers the floor of some of the hollows making it ideal for picnics, sun-tanning or just plain resting. In places along the shore, however, exploring walkers may be forced into waist-deep surf to skirt the occasional protruding rock.

"Wave sculptures are wonderful magnets to curiosity-seekers walking along the coast on a warm and sunny day. But they take on a more ominous role in the murky darkness of early evening or at dusk when a cloudless sky allows the moon to play its scary mind-games."

19

Not really expecting answers, Grandpa bent forward and lowered his voice to ask questions in a creepy stage whisper: "Is there someone or something around that inlet up ahead, lurking to pounce as I walk by? Did I just see a figure dart behind that stone pillar? Could that hole in the sandstone be the lair of a sea monster?"

"The sound of dripping water from the ceiling of the caves is heightened by its echo in the silence of the dark. Ocean-washed sun-parched roots dangle from overhanging sod at the top of the capes, uselessly eager to nourish dead and dying trees still upright along the hazardous ledge.

"Grey tree trunks entangled in the extended turf, long ago lifeless from earth erosion and sea-salt-blasting spray, hang upside down against the wall of the cape. Double-visioned by shadow-casting moonbeams, they sway in the wind in a grotesque puppet dance while awaiting their fate of being claimed by the patient sea."

Grandma wasn't paying too much attention to her husband's story, but as he spoke, Grandpa noticed the wide-eyed wonderment on the faces of the two very silent statues seated in front of him. He had set the mood and was now considering perhaps to ease up on the twinges of fear he may have created in the minds of his grandchildren. He also believed that most humans, especially the young, enjoy an occasional bout of fright. With little more thought, Grandpa decided to continue with the gruesome history of the capes.

Kildare Capes at Dusk

"As described by the Elder before they began their walk, thin, knee-high grass covered a large, flat clearing atop the steep escarpment. It was more than spacious enough to hold the number of animals expected to attend. Crisscrossed windfalls, tangled brush, and crowded trees surrounded the glade for hundreds of metres. It was exactly what was needed to obscure the sight of prying eyes and muffle any sound waves travelling toward keen ears. The open area of the unmarked and private property was difficult to access and was far enough away from the nearest roadway to discourage unwelcome or accidental intruders. Another discouragement, especially to scaredy-cats, was the rumoured connection of Kildare Capes to the supernatural and the ghosts of fishermen and other sailors long lost at sea.

"Kildare Capes has its fair share of horror and spooky tales, weird and eerie unearthly happenings, and maritime yarns of shipwrecks, bloodthirsty pirates, ghost ships and buried treasure. Some are true, particularly the account of the Yankee Gale and the havoc it wreaked in a storm back in October of 1851. Of the hundreds of mostly American schooners fishing mackerel in the Gulf of St. Lawrence during those two fateful days, 90 were wrecked and 160 men were battered to death, drowned or missing.

"The fierce winds and waves of that super-storm killed, smashed, blew and carried many of the bodies of men, along with the debris of wrecked ships, to the shores of PEI. Mangled bodies, tangled in seaweed and rope, were among the wooden pieces of ships, torn sails, barrels and other cargo. It was a horrendous greeting for the PEI land-clearing and potato farmers on the morning after the vicious gale.

"At Kildare Capes, three unidentified bodies found washed ashore were taken by horse and cart to a makeshift grave site in a nearby farmer's field. It was there they were wrapped together in sailcloth and buried in an unmarked grave. Their pit would eventually become part of a nearby official church burial ground, but it wasn't until 145 years later that gravediggers would accidentally uncover their bones.

"In the calming days after the deadly tempest, the waves of the sea brought the bodies of twelve more sailors to the shore of Kildare Capes. With no other place to take the grotesque and rotting bodies, local farmers carted these unfortunate and unknown souls for burial in the same makeshift graveyard. The exact location of these bodies has never been discovered and it has been said that their ghosts are doomed to wander the shore of Kildare Capes until they are properly put to rest.

Yankee Gale monument in church graveyard

"While surveying the site," continued Grandpa, "both Stompin' Tom and the Elder had noticed one thing that was obviously out-of-place – a grey,

23

granite boulder resting near the edge of the cape. The top of the huge rock was as flat and glossy as the ice of a freshly-Zambonied hockey rink. It sat on the ground perfectly level. Since no natural granite exists on PEI, where had it come from? Who had brought it? Why, when and how had they done so, and for what purpose?

Huge Flat-topped Granite Boulder

"Stompin' Tom was excited about the location and hoped they would be able to find a way to send messages to animals all across Canada from that point. As they stood beside the mysterious rock discussing the problem, and as if in response to their puzzle, a single gigantic wave, creating the sound of a savage roar by slamming itself against the cliff, rushed up the sandstone face, over the top lip, and drenched the couple with the remains of its whitecap.

"Even before Stompin' Tom and the Elder realized what it was that had soaked and knocked them backward a few steps, the rogue wave had already retreated into the calm of the ocean. It left behind only the bubbling sound of gently ebbing water, swishing in and around the rocks below as if nothing had happened.

"The immediate reaction of a startled and dripping Stompin' Tom was to blurt out, 'What the heck was all that about?' before he told Mathilda he thought he heard giggling coming from under the big rock. The wet but seemingly undeterred Mi'kmaq Elder, appearing even more enthused by the unusual happening, responded by saying she thought the sea had just sent them a message. She pointed out that the supernatural atmosphere at that spot was probably ideal for conjuring up Mi'kmaq spirits through *Glooscap*, their legendary leader of the spirit world."

"The Mi'kmaq Elder went on to say she believed *Glooscap* may have just shown them he had already made contact with the *Pukulatamuj* (pook-oo-lah-tuh-mooch). She described them as tiny spirits that live in rocky places and possess strong magical powers. She also added that the little ones didn't usually harm humans and were fond of playing harmless but occasionally annoying tricks on people.

"While mumbling his displeasure as he tipped the water off the brim

25

of his cowboy hat, Stompin' Tom reaffirmed to the Elder that he had heard something near the rock. Deep inside he not only felt somewhat mystified, but pleased and more confident of a positive outcome of their project.

"The drenched Elder, anxious to get into dry clothing, attempted to assure Stompin' Tom that she would be fine walking alone on an immediate return trip to her SUV. She insisted he remain until he had examined the place to his satisfaction. But Stompin' Tom was too much of a gentleman to have her return without an escort, so the two set off on foot, sloshing downhill together to where their vehicles were parked.

"In parting, Elder Mathilda said she would contact Stompin' Tom when the perfect day arrived to conduct a communication experiment with the animals. She also informed him she would attempt to arrange for the use of the property and reminded him of the name Windrail bestowed upon the land by the owner. Then, after reminding him to come alone when she called and to be sure to bring his guitar, she drove away toward her home on Lennox Island."

CHAPTER FOUR

THE SIXTH SENSE

Here's a question for you," said Grandpa, seeming to go off topic and bringing everyone's mind back to the living room. "Can anyone tell me our five basic senses?"

The room came alive as both Traedan and Emma shouted out answers and were able, between the two of them, to come up with all five.

"You got them all," Grandpa proudly told his grandkids, "I remember them by 'three snakes between two trees' or just TSSST."

As if the grandchildren needed emphasis, he stuck out his tongue, pointed to it and started identifying the sense organs of his body, his finger jabbing all over his face as he called them out:

"**T**aste (tongue), **S**mell (nose), **S**ound (ears), **S**ight (eyes), and **T**ouch (skin). All are connected and send information to our brain. One of their many purposes is to help us communicate with other beings, including animals."

Then, acting as if he was about to tell a huge secret, Grandpa added, "But did you know that some people believe there may be a sixth sense? I'll talk about that as soon as we take a break for drinks, popcorn and a pee."

When everyone was refreshed, restocked and resettled after the break, Grandpa returned to his story.

"Do you remember when I told you about my old dog, Sporty? How he used to get nervous, run upstairs and hide under my bed long before we knew we would soon be getting a thunderstorm?"

"Hey! My cat does the same thing!" burst out Emma as she jumped up from the couch, causing a few puffed kernels of corn to scatter. "And every time we looked for her, we never could find out where she went to hide!"

"Well," said Grandpa, "Many animals seem to be able to sense something is about to occur long before humans realize it. A few years ago, on the day a huge tsunami slammed against the shore of a country in Asia called Indonesia, many birds, monkeys, dogs and other creatures had all been acting strangely. They knew something unusual was about to happen. Up to an hour before the massive wave hit, many animals, including elephants, were already running for the hills. A lot of animals saved themselves by doing so, but tens of thousands of people died because they were unaware of, and unprepared for, the coming deadly swell of seawater.

"I don't know if we can call it a sixth sense, but animal behaviour experts and scientists agree that many animals can hear and feel things we humans cannot. Some of their sensory abilities are far sharper than ours so they can sense things a lot sooner than humans.

"Stompin' Tom must have also been aware of this so-called sixth sense that many animals seem to possess. He must have felt confident that the blue whales in the Gulf of St. Lawrence near Windrail would be able to transmit messages to the marine mammals living along Canada's three ocean coasts. At times, whales speak to each other in frequencies too low for humans to hear. These sounds can carry through the water for long distances. The whales also know the locations of sound channels in the oceans that permit them to communicate for even greater distances, sometimes for thousands of kilometres. Could this have been the way marine mammals in the sea were told about *The Secret Meeting Place*?" wondered Grandpa rhetorically.

"Vibrations can travel through the earth like waves. Dogs, cats, snakes, horses and rodents are only some of the animals known to feel early vibrations underground or on land – such as the faintest tremble of an upcoming earthquake or volcano – far in advance of people. Snakes seem to be best at this since their entire bodies, including their head, is usually close to the ground. If quaking messages were pounded on the ground at Windrail, could it not be possible for them to reach inland lake and river animals, and those in their dens, burrows, mountains and forests? Could the message about *The Secret Meeting Place* have been sent to land animals all across Canada through vibrations?" he questioned without expecting an answer.

"Seeming to have covered the animals on land and in the sea, Stompin' Tom would then have been left to concentrate on animals in the air. Those would be the birds of Canada as well as bats, the only mammals that can fly. His only challenge now was to see if the winds and wind turbines at North Cape could assist by relaying sound waves through the air."

"Does anyone know how many degrees there are in a circle?" Grandpa suddenly asked, as if to keep everyone on their toes.

This time Traedan beat his little sister to the answer by exclaiming, "360 degrees!"

29

"That's right, Traedan, and North Cape, PEI is exposed to wind in 300 of those degrees over open sea. That's almost a complete circle and one of the main reasons why it was selected by the government for an experimental wind testing site and wind turbine farm.

Nature and technology can exist in perfect harmony. All the wind turbines at the farm were built to automatically swivel their blades to face the slightest whisper of a breeze. They are capable of facing in the direction of any one of Canada's ten provinces and three territories at any time of night or day."

"North Cape and its namesake lighthouse sit at the northwestern tip of PEI where the waters of the Gulf of St. Lawrence meet the waters of Northumberland Strait. This borderline, separating the Gulf and the Strait, is the longest natural rock reef in North America, stretching northward from shore for two kilometres. Because of the reef's danger to ships, the North Cape lighthouse was built – in the year Canada was born – as a warning beacon for sailors. Can anyone tell me what year that was?"

"In 1867," replied Emma and Traedan together. "That's an easy one!"

Grandpa gave them a wink and thumbs up as he continued on.

"Exposed during low tide, the reef is a favourite gathering place for many marine birds and seals, and a delightful stroll for explorers and nature lovers like us. We'll have to add it to our list of Things To See and Do and walk along it as far as we can someday soon," he added. "But let's get back to Windrail to see if Stompin' Tom and Elder Mathilda were able to solve the problem of sending messages through the air."

North Cape Wind Turbines, Lighthouse, Reef

CHAPTER FIVE

NORTH CAPE

It was early afternoon when Stompin' Tom was called to meet once more with Mi'kmaq Elder Mathilda at Windrail. As she had directed, he had come alone and, as usual, was dressed in black from cowboy hat to western boots. This time, he had decided to take the shorter distance between the highway and *The Secret Meeting Place*.

"Now listen closely to this lesson, grandkids," said a grinning Grandpa. "Stompin' Tom would soon be reminded that the shortest distance between two points is only shorter if it can be travelled in a straight line."

"Stompin' Tom had left his black Chevy Silverado pickup truck parked on the North Cape Coastal Drive Highway and was meandering through the slapping saplings and alders, struggling to follow a barely visible path as it snaked through the tall trees. Habitually, he would be carrying his guitar by its neck over his right shoulder but today it was inside its case dangling from his left hand, protected from scratching twigs and thorny undergrowth. In his right hand he clutched his stompin' board, a last minute decision he had made to bring the piece of plywood along. He was glad he had done so because he was now using it to shield his face from being whacked by lower branches and stinging spruce needles. Even so, by the time he reached the outer edge of the clearing, he was a bit winded from stepping and crawling over the many windfalls and had added a few more minor cuts and scratches to his tough, rugged hide.

"Stompin' Tom was amazed by the silence. He hadn't heard or seen anyone or anything else around even while crossing the grassy clearing. Now, as he leaned against a weathered old maple flagpole a few metres from the flat-topped rock, he wondered why the only sound he could hear was the waters of the gulf giving a gentle foot-massage to the capes.

"Deep in thought, he was more than a bit startled when he heard *Kwe* (Hello) behind him and instinctively twisted around to see a human form emerging from the shadows of the woods. It was Elder Mathilda and when she came into sight he couldn't help but notice how beautifully dressed and stately she appeared in the colourful traditional clothes of her People."

Mi'kmaq Elder
in Traditional Dress

"After an exchange of greetings, the Elder informed Stompin' Tom that she had obtained permission from its anonymous owner to use Windrail as a gathering place. She went on to say he still would not disclose any details about the unusual rock they were standing beside. She added he believed it may be connected to, or somehow associated with, the government Wind Testing Site and Wind Turbine Farm at North Cape.

"Mathilda told Stompin' Tom that, according to the owner, if you drew a straight line from the flat rock to the magnetic north pole, it would pass directly through the large main experimental wind turbine and the lighthouse at North Cape. She said he also told her that the distance between the North Cape experimental wind turbine and the rock is supposed to be exactly 20 kilometres as the crow flies."

Now it was Grandma's turn to interrupt Grandpa's story and get involved. Sensing her grandchildren may be somewhat confused, she leaned forward, brushed away a few snack-food crumbs, and placed her iPad on the coffee table in front of them. After clicking until she located her compass application (app), she began to give out directions.

"Let's pretend this coffee table is the flat rock at Windrail," said Grandma. "I'm going to turn my iPad until the compass needle is pointing to the 'N' which stands for North." She then told Emma to place a page from a small, yellow, sticky notepad on the wall across the room exactly where the compass needle was pointing.

"Grandpa, go and stand in front of the sticky note that Emma stuck onto the wall and pretend you're the *old* North Cape lighthouse," she directed, smiling as she stressed the 'old' and getting a wink back from the old man in return.

"Traedan, you can be the huge experimental wind turbine and we'll pretend you're twenty kilometres away from the rock. Stand directly in line between the compass on the coffee table and your Grandpa. Now you don't have to hold out your arms like wind turbine blades unless you wish to keep them that way. Emma, please check to make sure your brother and Grandpa are in a straight line."

34

As soon as everyone understood and had a good picture in their mind of the rock, wind turbine and lighthouse in a straight line with the magnetic north pole, Grandma turned her attention back to solitaire and Grandpa resumed his story.

"I don't believe anyone could blame Stompin' Tom if he had begun to get a bit doubtful about being able to communicate with the animals across Canada," continued Grandpa, "But he was also as anxious as the Elder when she suggested they should see what would happen if he stood on the mysterious flat rock and sang a Stompin' song.

"But first, acts of preparation had to be performed."

CHAPTER SIX

MAPLES AND SMUDGING

T he instrument case Stompin' Tom had carried through the snarled woods to the clearing at Windrail didn't contain his usual Gibson guitar," said Grandpa as he returned to his story.

"Isn't that the same name as on your guitar over there, Grandpa?" interrupted, Traedan, pointing to the one used when they all sang *The Hockey Song.*

"You're very observant, Traedan. You must have inherited those special powers from your police detective father," replied Grandpa. "Yes, they're both made by the same company but mine is a much less expensive model. For this important occasion though, Stompin' Tom had chosen to bring a guitar he had received as a gift made especially for him.

"When Stompin' Tom removed what he sometimes called his axe from its protective case, it was a dazzling sight to behold. Reinforcing what he referred to as his east to west Canada-wide Stompin' Grounds, the six-string

36

instrument was made from two types of maple – Hard Rock Maple from the Maritimes to give it extra sound energy, wrapped in the beautiful woodgrain of Big Leaf Maple from BC. To top it off, a red Canadian maple leaf sticker on the headstock above the words, A Proud Canadian, said it all."

"Reaching back into the case, Stompin' Tom pulled out a neatly folded Canadian Maple Leaf flag. Using two metal guitar strings from the set of spares he always carried, he attached and hoisted our Nation's iconic banner to flutter atop the nearby maple pole. He crossed his fingers and hoped aloud that a brisk wind wouldn't come up and snap the flagstaff's frayed old rope, or even the weather-beaten mast itself.

"From early years the maple leaf has been worldly recognized as a symbol of Canada and moreso since it was adopted by Canadians on February 15th, 1965 as the main feature of our official flag. Since our flag doesn't display a connection with any other country, it is truly Canadian and ours alone.

"Stompin' Tom then wondered if he should use his stompin' board. He told Elder Mathilda it had been a last minute decision to bring it along since he didn't think he would have to worry about his boot scratching the top of the rock."

"Elder Mathilda laughed at his joke and reaffirmed he wouldn't be 'The Stomper' without it."

"The signature stompin' board usually used by Stompin' Tom was simply a piece of plywood. Its purpose was to prevent damage to a stage floor while he kept the beat by stomping his left heel in time to the song he was singing. The wooden piece he carried with him to Windrail, however, had been intentionally cut from a sheet made from one of Canada's ten native maple tree species.

"Stompin' Tom gently set his guitar on the stompin' board he had placed atop the flat rock, then nodded his readiness to Elder Mathilda to include those items in her smudging ritual. She had been waiting nearby with a fan of eagle feathers in one hand representing the air and its feathered creatures, and a large smouldering scallop shell as a smudge bowl in the other to represent the ocean and its aquatic inhabitants. Earth and its occupiers would be acknowledged by the ashes of the plants being burned. She had arrived dressed for the occasion and was now fully prepared to perform a smudging ceremony in Mi'kmaq tradition to cleanse the mind, body and spirit as well as bless the special objects.

"With *Glooscap* as their spiritual guide, the Mi'kmaq People lived a simple life in harmony and respect with nature and animals. In gratitude, the Elder had wisely chosen to burn sweetgrass with which to please the spirits. Smoke would also flow from the bowl from two additional plant choices – sage for the protection of the humans and animals involved in the project, and cedar as a cleanser to get rid of any negativity and replace it with positive energy.

"If Elder Mathilda was concerned about not being able to get the attention of her People's cultural hero, she needn't have worried. As soon as she began her smudging ceremony, a shrill cry from *Kwimu* (Kwee-moo), a loon on a nearby pond, sliced through the silence. In Mi'kmaq lore, the

Kwimu plays the role of messenger and its cry immediately reports the activities of humans to *Glooscap*. Unknowingly to the Elder and Stompin' Tom, all their movements were being closely watched.

"Using the eagle feather as a fan, Elder Mathilda performed her smudging routine by gently waving the smoke over the maple guitar and stompin' board as well as the huge boulder. That seemed to stir up the tiny *Pukulatamuj* noisily rustling about unseen in the tall grass around the bottom of the rock. With his open hands, Stompin' Tom fanned the smoke in his direction and over his sense organs."

"Remember T-S-S-S-T?" Grandpa unexpectedly blurted out. The sudden outburst caused his grandchildren to jerk to attention from their relaxed drowsy state and Grandma to nearly drop her iPad. It also resulted in a disapproving frown aimed at her hubby. Hiding a mischievous grin, Grandpa went on as if nothing had happened.

"Stompin' Tom completed his self-smudging with a washing motion to bring the smoke over his hands, head and heart from the scallop shell held by the Elder. When the ceremony was over, he felt ready to test the communication system and the animals' reaction to a song. He was very curious to know how far away it would be picked up by their keen senses.

"The tune he chose was fittingly called *Land of the Maple Tree.* It described Canada's majesty from Newfoundland and Labrador to BC, and the country's spectacular diversity between the Great Lakes and North Pole. It told of the first meetings between Indigenous People and the newcomers – fishermen, *coureur de bois*, trappers, prospectors, explorers, homesteaders

39

and woodsmen. It related how they all came together to form a legacy, to stand up for freedom and a culture we can proudly call our own. The song also paid tribute to a beautiful and tranquil land where we can still roam free in harmony with nature and its animals.

"Taking his guitar in hand, Stompin' Tom leapt up onto the flat rock and positioned his feet on the stompin' board. He selected the 'A' chord, strummed the strings to check if his instrument was in tune and then, satisfied, he began to play."

Grandpa just couldn't resist the opportunity to perform before his captive audience. He picked up his nearby Gibson and sang the entire first verse:

> Where the Coureur de Bois met the Iroquois,
> The Micmac and the Cree,
> The Trapper and the Woodsman came
> And left this legacy;
> To roam the woods, to fish and hunt
> And always to be free,
> And to stand up for our Culture
> In the LAND OF THE MAPLE TREE. ©

Stompin' Tom on the Flat-topped Granite Rock
Illustration by T.L. "Skippy" Drew

CHAPTER SEVEN

TERRIFYING SCREAMS

As soon as Stompin' Tom began his trademark stomping during his song, PEI's noisy provincial bird, the blue jay, sprang out on flailing wings from its hiding place in the boughs of a nearby spruce tree. Within seconds, after assessing the situation and realizing that no threat existed, the jay confidently returned to its normal squawking lifestyle. That action cued the other animals that all was well and caused the meadow to come to life like an exploding overblown balloon.

"Within the clearing, a red fox and its silver cousin, began bouncing up and down as if on a trampoline to peek above the tall grass. A usually shy rabbit hopped out of the bushes to see firsthand what was going on while a chipmunk and squirrel ran up and down the trees in excitement. A skunk passed through unseen but certainly not undetected. *Pee-yew!* And a raccoon, usually asleep during the day, was shaken awake by all the ruckus. A garter snake, slithering along a log after crawling out from its underground pit home, was quick to divert its attention in the direction of the piercing sound of a spring peeper frog. The chaos in the clearing caused a curious old moss-raking horse in a distant farmyard to whinny in wonderment, instantly followed by the lonesome howl of a coyote emerging from its den of pups in the far off woods.

"As Stompin' Tom continued to play, sing and stomp along, he remembered how oddly silent and seemingly devoid of life he had found their chosen spot upon his arrival. It was now confirmed that what he had believed to be abandonment was actually the animals' cautious reaction to their 'sixth sense' – that something unusual was about to occur. They had simply kept themselves out of sight until they were able to determine if it was safe to return to their normal lifestyle.

"While singing his selected song, Stompin' Tom would occasionally glance over the cape and across the waters of the Gulf of St. Lawrence. For that he was rewarded by spotting a pair of curious grey seals popping their heads out of the water and staring in his direction. But the most magnificent sight to catch his eye lasted only seconds. It was that of a huge breaching whale, rising above the waves and clapping its fins as if giving applause to the performer on the flat-topped rock atop the distant cape.

Breaching Humpback Whale

Grey Seal

"When he was about halfway through, Stompin' Tom was feeling pretty good about his song. It acknowledged the willingness of the Indigenous People, centuries ago, to share their knowledge, technology and innovations, specially-suited for travel throughout our vast True North

43

Wonderland, with the newcomers. The list included dog-teams, birch-bark canoes, snowshoes and toboggans. In the far north, the Inuit produced the kayak and saved lives by having taught many cheechako Arctic travellers how to quickly build an igloo for shelter during a blizzard. And even today, parkas handmade by the mainly Inuit women of the Arctic have the ability, yet to be matched by modern commercial manufacturers, to provide warmth and comfort during the coldest and wildest of northern winter snowstorms.

"The song also paid tribute to the sacrifices of Canada's animals in providing people with food, fuel, clothing and tools. The people benefitted from the sacrifices but in too many instances it was shamefully unnecessary, wasteful and environmentally unfriendly. Nature's scheme of things was knocked off balance when the bison were hunted to near extinction merely for sport or when they were considered to be nuisances to ranchers and railroad travel. Another reason perhaps, was to forcefully encourage Indigenous People to raise cattle on designated lands rather than to traditionally rely on bison meat to survive. Similarly, to name a few, beavers, otters, mink, muskrats, martin, foxes and wolves were over-trapped during the fur trade as Europeans satisfied a vain desire to wear the latest in fur fashions.

"By the time Stompin' Tom neared the final chorus of his song, he was fully aware that something was amiss. Glancing over at Elder Mathilda, he could see the concerned look on her face as well. From the response of the local animals it was obvious that the vibrations emanating from his stomping were travelling across the land and underground as expected. It also appeared from the reaction of the ocean dwellers, that sound waves were being created in the waters of the sea. But, except for that spying loon, the boisterous blue jay and a local murder of crows that were within the range of his voice, no birds were being affected by his performance. Several times as he played, he had observed flocks of seagulls and cormorants flying high overhead without displaying any reaction to what was occurring below them. Obviously, the sound waves of his voice weren't reaching North Cape 20 kilometres to the north from where they could be distributed all across Canada. It was just too far away.

"Elder Mathilda was as disappointed as Stompin' Tom at the outcome but she still felt optimistic that *Glooscap* would seek the help of the gigantic spirit wind bird, *Wuchowsen* (wuh-joo-sen). The folklore of her People included stories of its enormous wings being capable of producing winds from soft, warm zephyrs to howling hurricanes. Perhaps *Wuchowsen* could be of help in forcing sound waves through the air from the flat rock at Windrail to the wind turbines at North Cape.

"It was during the sixth and final verse of *Land of the Maple Tree*, with still no reaction from any winged animals, that a horrifying, blood-curdling shriek, loud and long, came from the bushes at the closest edge of the clearing. The animals scattered in all directions. Startled, Stompin' Tom's guitar, boot and heart all skipped beats as he recoiled and promptly fell off the edge of the rock. At that very moment, as he lay on his back temporarily stunned by shocking surprise, a massive shadow made by the wings of a monstrous raptor, swooped low above him. The whoosh of a powerful gust of wind followed the phantom fowl as it rose sharply then disappeared over the treeline.

"Elder Mathilda rushed over to Stompin' Tom's side to check on his condition. Finding him to be unhurt, she whispered her belief that the giant bird was *Wuchowsen* and was sure it had come to help.

"Stompin' Tom rose slowly to his feet. Recalling the earlier drenching by the rogue wave at Windrail, he groaned that the Mi'kmaq spirits just might become the death of him.

"His life on the road over the years had provided Stompin' Tom with the opportunity – intended or otherwise – to spend the occasional night alone in the wilderness bordering some of the long, remote stretches of the Trans Canada Highway. As such, he had been hardened to accept many of the unexplained and unidentifiable weird noises that arose during the night to interrupt his sleep and sometimes scare the heck out of him. But this one was different. It sounded too inanimate and not of this earth to describe.

"During those few seconds while Stompin' Tom was regaining his senses and composure, the shrill, hair-raising wail came to a drawn-out, fading end. Once his head had cleared, he cautiously began to approach the edge of the concealing thicket where the demonic sound seemed to have originated. In his mind he wondered if someone or something had hurt themselves, or worse, had been hurt by someone or something. He didn't know what he was about to find hidden within the shadows of the underbrush. Would it be human or even animal? But curiosity and the need to help someone who may be in distress, urged him on. The silence was unnerving. Creeping forward, he crouched and – ever so carefully – began to untangle and remove the intertwined clump of shrubs, branches, vines, and grass concealing the object.

"Whatever it was, was about his height. As he worked at removing the entangling foliage, Stompin' Tom's sudden jerky movements caused another screech. Once again, he reacted by stepping back, but this time he rebounded and grabbed the thing firmly in hand. The screaming stopped.

"Then Stompin' Tom began to laugh. So, too, did the Elder. She had been right behind him all the while, watching his back and prepared to assist. Their laughter was a combination of relief and delight as they stared at the metal contraption in front of them that looked like a windmill. The eerie sounds had been metal scraping against metal. Its propeller blades had been forced to turn slightly from the powerful gust of wind made by the wings of the big diving bird. Because of *Wuchowsen,* Stompin' Tom and Elder Mathilda had just uncovered and freed an air-blowing fan from its prison of brush.

"The valiant fan had tried its best to help send Stompin' Tom's song and music waves to the large experimental wind turbine at North Cape. Unfortunately, it wasn't able to free itself from the vines strangling its blades and the corrosion gripping its moving parts. It was the blast of wind from *Wuchowsen's* gusty power dive that had supplied enough additional force to cause a partial turn of the blowing fan's vanes. The sudden movement had created the terrifying noise that led to its discovery. Even so, Stompin' Tom was so impressed with the wind-maker's determination to do its job that he likened it to *The Little Engine That Could* and named it Noisy Nick.

"After clearing Noisy Nick of all flora, Stompin' Tom noticed that the bottom ends of its four-legged frame had been welded onto two parallel lengths of railway tracks. The weight and length of the iron rails kept Noisy Nick upright, level, and sturdy. Without special equipment, it would have been humanly impossible to move the heavy structure out of position.

"Stamped into each rail was the original logo of the Canadian Pacific Railway (CPR). The design displayed maple leaves and a beaver, both easily recognizable Canadian symbols known throughout the world. The crest paid tribute to those special rodents for their importance in the early development of our country. Obviously, someone had obtained possession of the old original iron tracks after the CPR switched its line to much harder and stronger rails made of steel.

Early logo of the CPR

"Stompin' Tom's discovery of the logo impressions brought back memories of his boyhood spent in school at Skinners Pond. In history class he had learned of the challenging feat of engineering undertaken by Canadians in the late 19th century in building the CPR, their first transcontinental railway. One of its purposes was to connect Canada and its people. Another was to entice British Columbia (BC), a British colony back then, to join the Dominion of Canada. BC agreed and in 1871 it became the sixth, the largest and the westernmost province of Canada. British Columbia was then no longer British, but no one bothered to change its name and it remains a misnomer to this day. History also implies that there was no input by Indigenous People into the name or ownership of the unceded territory.

"When the historic Last Spike was driven into the completed railroad at Craigellachie, BC, it connected the Canadian provinces from the Atlantic to the Pacific Oceans. In the famous picture of that event, one small boy is at the ceremony and people, even today, still wonder who he was and why he wasn't in school."

The Last Spike, Craigellachie, BC

"On his treks across the land he called his stompin' grounds," said Grandpa to his grandkids, "I'm sure Stompin' Tom became familiar with many of the thousands of kilometres of track that make up the CPR."

Then, bringing everyone's mind back to Windrail and Noisy Nick, Grandpa returned to his story.

"When Stompin' Tom examined Noisy Nick's fan, he noticed it had only two blades instead of the three required of a wind turbine. Another difference was the hub on which the blades spun. It was solidly attached to the body and unable to swing around to face the wind. Since Noisy Nick was too heavy to move, the wind coming from only one direction would be

49

effective.

"That feature prompted Stompin' Tom to use the compass app on his cell phone to check the position of the wind-making fan. He set the cellphone down on the flat rock and turned it until the compass needle pointed north. It confirmed that Noisy Nick was standing directly in line with the flat rock, North Cape and the Magnetic North Pole.

"The newfound wind-maker would work at its highest efficiency when the fan spun and a south wind blew. Together they would increase the speed and distance of any sound waves, such as those from a Stompin' Tom song, originating from atop the flat rock. When the wind was blowing from any other direction, or not at all, Noisy Nick could provide its own southerly breeze by using battery power. One had been attached to the wind-making machine along with a solar panel to keep it electrically charged by the sun.

"It was just as Grandma demonstrated to us earlier," Grandpa reminded everyone. "Let's line up again, and this time Emma will take the place of Noisy Nick in our very straight lineup."

After the short demonstration, Grandpa continued on:

"Elder Mathilda and Stompin' Tom still had no idea what type of experimentation the government had been conducting at the North Cape Wind Energy Institute, and probably never would, but they now knew how Windrail got its name – a combination of **wind**-making fan and **rail**way track.

"Stompin' Tom retrieved a jar of Vaseline from his guitar case. His wandering lifestyle had taught him to keep a few necessities always handy.

One was band-aids, another petroleum jelly. The latter especially, was good for anything from chapped lips, rashes and insect bites to lubricating rusty moving metal parts and a host of other things too numerous to mention.

"By the time Stompin' Tom applied the lubricant and had the rusty blades turning practically noiselessly, Elder Mathilda was already prepared to perform a smudging ceremony on their newfound machine. They were leaving nothing to chance."

Noisy Nick Illustration by T.L. "Skippy" Drew

CHAPTER EIGHT

NOISY NICK

No sooner had Elder Mathilda completed the smudging ceremony, when a change in the wind produced a groan from Noisy Nick. Stompin' Tom wasted no time in jumping onto his rock perch and beginning, once again, to play, sing and stomp *Land of the Maple Tree*. The wind was now blowing directly from the south and as he performed, several scratching sounds and moans were heard from the direction of the fan as the two-bladed propeller jerked its way around to complete its first full cycle. Before long, with the Vaseline well spread, it was spinning at top speed, free of the choking grasp of vegetation and the clutches of corrosion that had kept it quiet for so long.

"Perfectly in line with the flat rock on which Stompin' Tom was performing and because sound travels further with the wind, the propeller on Noisy Nick was tilted slightly upward to where winds travel even faster. It was doing its best to ensure the sound waves carrying Stompin' Tom's song would reach the huge experimental wind turbine site at North Cape, 20 kilometres away.

"There doesn't appear to be any official record of what happened next but rumour has it," said Grandpa, "that some of the government workers at North Cape were freaking out with alarm when they noticed all the wind turbines spinning for a few minutes at close to their top speed of 90 kilometres per hour. Taking advantage of the air flow made by the wake or wash behind the propellers, not only were they all whirling at the same time but while facing in different directions! The sound waves of the song Stompin' Tom was performing were blowing in every degree of a circle and being relayed to cover all of Canada.

A few people at the Wind Farm ran for safety, wondering if they were inside the eye of a hurricane. Trembling in fear, they watched in wide-eyed silence as a monstrous feathered creature, having completed its magical moment, circled overhead, climbed higher and higher skyward, then disappeared from sight.

"Somehow sensing the song was meant for them, the local animals began returning to the meadow. This time the collection included many different types of birds and none flew by without reacting to the music being made below them.

"Even before he finished singing, Stompin' Tom's cellphone had begun to ring and record messages. Earlier, he had arranged for friends in the farthest reaches of Canada's north, south, east and west to report any changes they may see in animal activity or unusual behaviour at their location. The news they sent back was good.

"At Cape Columbia on Ellesmere Island, Nunavut, Canada's most northerly point of land, muskoxen, walruses, and the territory's official bird, the rock ptarmigan whose feathers turn white in winter, were expressing excitement and curiosity. The white wolves, called the Ghosts of the Arctic, were on an unusual howling spree and the usually docile muskoxen were butting heads and kicking up their heels. The Arctic jaegers, known as the bird pirates of the sea, had stopped stealing from other birds and were silently staring out across the ocean waters, while a herd of tooth-clicking walruses became a group of rubbernecking bobbleheads.

Ghost of the Arctic **Muskox** **Ptarmigan**

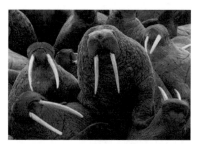

Arctic Jaeger **Walruses**

"The southernmost piece of land in Canada is Middle Island, Ontario. It's in Lake Erie and part of Point Pelee National Park. Of the many birds suddenly becoming disturbed and unsettled was a large flock of wild turkeys that had taken refuge in the treetops and become engaged in a non-stop chorus of gobbledygook. A more than normal number of rare hermit warblers and black swifts also stopped in as if to catch up on the latest news.

Hermit Warbler

Point Pelee Wild Turkey

Black Swift

"The easternmost point in Canada is the historic lighthouse at Cape Spear, Newfoundland and Labrador near the provincial capital of St. John's. The province is a birdwatcher's paradise. On this day, hundreds of species with names such as murres, razorbills and puffins appeared to be more plentiful, excited and wary following Stompin' Tom's song.

Razorbill

Puffin

Murre

"Canada's westernmost location is the Yukon-Alaska border near Mount Logan, our nation's highest peak. It would be a long, tough hike for anyone to get there so Stompin' Tom had asked a friend in Haida Gwaii to provide an animal report. Formerly called the Queen Charlottes, and often referred to as the Canadian Galapagos, the group of about 150 western islands are the most isolated in Canada. Secluded evolution over thousands of years has created several unique subspecies of animals found nowhere else on earth. Included are the biggest black bears in the world, dusky shrews, ermine, pine martens and stoats. Flying animals in the far west included bats and the endangered trumpeter swans. One of the many bald eagles spotted by the reporter appeared to be discussing the matter with a raven over dinner.

Silver-haired Bat

Endangered Trumpeter Swan

Bald Eagle and Raven

"From all reports, it seemed that a means of communicating with the animals on land, through water and now also in the air, had been accomplished. *Wuchowsen*, the spirit wind bird, had done its job well."

CHAPTER NINE

EVIL MONSTERS

Grandma returned to the living-room with blankets she had fetched after noticing a bit of a chill in the early evening. She handed them out to her grandchildren and helped them turn themselves into overwrapped mummies comfy and warm on the couch. As soon as they appeared snuggled and content, Grandpa went on to describe some of Canada's human-eating ogres.

"The very first night that a south wind blew following the successful wind-making test, Stompin' Tom and Elder Mathilda arrived at Windrail to find a surprise awaiting them. Where once stood a drab and weather-beaten structure was a bright and shiny Noisy Nick, newly-painted in Canada's official colours of red and white. It stood softly gleaming in the moon-glow, glinting here and there as Stompin' Tom scanned its entire body with a flashlight beam to aid his inspection. When the battery switch was flipped on, the now glossy silver fan blades sprang into action and purred like Emma's kitten. Every part of Noisy Nick had been cleaned and painted. Even the grass around it had been manicured to perfection. When they heard faint giggles coming from the direction of the big flat rock, Stompin' Tom realized what Elder Mathilda had already suspected – it was the result of hard work by the occasionally mischievous *Pukulatamuj*, the tiny rock spirits. Stompin'

Tom turned and expressed his appreciation in the dwarfs' direction while Elder Mathilda graciously said her thanks. Standing proudly nearby, Noisy Nick was noisy no more.

"That same night, an announcement of the date, time and place of the gathering to resolve the matter of Canada's Big Five list, was tele-stomped to the animals," said Grandpa. "Stompin' Tom had decided to send future messages very late at night after hearing about the commotion at North Cape during the first trial.

"To avoid a huge gathering of spectators, only the representatives selected by the creatures — one per species — would be permitted to attend.

"After the invitations were sent out, Stompin' Tom and Elder Mathilda were saying their goodbyes and about to depart when Elder Mathilda added one final concern to Stompin' Tom's agenda. She mentioned to him that up until now they had only been dealing with the happy, cooperative and accommodating traditional spirits of the Mi'kmaq People. She thought that for the sake of the safety of the animals and humans involved, he should also be aware of those that may do harm. The Elder then went on to describe two of the most dangerous Mi'kmaq spirits.

"She told him about the *Kukwes* (kook-wess), a kind of human-eating ogre. He's greedy, hairy and has a bear-like head. The other is *Jipijka'm* (chih-pitch-kawm), an underwater snake with one, two-coloured horn. Also said to eat humans, it's sometimes called the unicorn serpent.

"Mention of horrifying ghostly creatures immediately brought *Wendigo* to my mind," said Grandpa. "That evil spirit is from the folklore of the Algonquin First Nations and is believed to prowl the eastern and central wilderness areas of Canada in search of human flesh. To my knowledge, Stompin' Tom never had an encounter with a *Wendigo* on his many hitchhiking trips across our nation. Not even when it was necessary for him to spend an occasional night alone in a roadside ditch. I have, however, heard many stories of the evil spirit's hungry search for lost fishermen, hunters, mushroom pickers, campers, hikers and lonely travellers.

"The *Wendigo* has been described as having pointed animal-like ears and antlers or horns sprouting from its head. Apparently yellowish skin and matted hair covers its powerful body and even though it's gigantic, its body odour permits it to be smelled long before it's seen. The demon's eyes are sunken and glow like hot coals in a campfire. Sharp, pointy, yellow teeth are inside a mouth already full of a long tongue and bad breath. If *Wendigo* sneaks into a campsite cloaked in the night mist, those of us careless enough to have let our campfires die out are soon snatched up, never to be seen again," cautioned Grandpa. "Fortunately, PEI is not known to be within the *Wendigo's* stalking range."

With those words, Grandpa returned to his story and the dangers that two of the Mi'kmaq spirits might bring to the meeting.

"Stompin' Tom thanked the Elder for the warning. After giving serious thought to the situation, he believed that the threat would be low. He and the Elder would be the only humans involved and the animals were excellent at taking care of themselves. Nevertheless, it was his responsibility to provide safety and protection to those on the land atop the capes at *The Secret Meeting Place* and in the sea directly below.

Canadian Wendigo

"Then a thought suddenly struck him.............of course. Sasha!

"Stompin' Tom decided to contact a humanoid creature he had literally bumped into out in BC some time ago. He wondered if a *Sasquatch* would be willing to help him out."

At this moment in his story, Grandpa rose from his lazy-boy chair and plopped himself down in a sitting position on the floor in front of his hushed and attentive grandchildren. Lowering his voice to just above a whisper he continued his tale in a low tone of secrecy as two serious faces with very wide eyes stared back at him.

"Hundreds of communities of the various nations of the Inuit, First Nations and Métis, speaking in many different tongues, make up the Indigenous People in Canada. Some of their beliefs, customs and stories, passed through the generations, are similar. These include their traditional spirits which tend to show a close relationship between humans and animals. Of their many mythical creatures, at least two have become such legends in Canadian folklore that they may actually exist.

"For centuries the Coast Salish First Nations of the Fraser Valley in BC have told stories of chance encounters with a human-like animal covered in hair that walks upright. They called the beast *Sasquatch*, which means 'wild man' in their language. Reports of *Sasquatch* sightings, unexpected meetings with fishermen, hunters, hikers and campers, and huge footprint discoveries, continue even to this day. But a *Sasquatch* has never been found dead, or captured alive, or photographed clearly, so positive proof of its existence has never been determined. After hearing my story, it will be up to you to believe or disbelieve in its existence."

As Grandpa finished speaking, Emma, with a tiny shiver and a bit of a quiver in her voice, questioned, "Wha...what's the second mythical creature, Grandpa?"

"They call it *Ogopogo* and I'll tell you about her right after *Sasquatch*," he answered."

Sasquatch Illustration by Evan D. Maksymchuk

CHAPTER TEN

SASHA SASQUATCH

O n a snow-capped mountain peak in the wilds of BC," began Grandpa to Traedan and Emma, "Sasha Sasquatch was enjoying a cool, sunny day of kiteboarding when the white powdery snow beneath him began to shake. It was the secret signal! He had been expecting the tremors and knew at once it was his call to come to *The Secret Meeting Place.*

"When the shaking stopped, what Sasha hadn't expected was the whumpfing sound of collapsing snow closer to the top of the mountain. He looked up in time to see the shooting cracks on the snow-packed surface and knew an avalanche was about to occur.

"He quickly buckled himself to his huge red and white Canadian

Maple Leaf-designed kite before bending down to attach his huge feet to his snowboard. As he hurriedly strapped his long tootsies onto the board, Sasha was reminded by their size why many humans called him Bigfoot.

"Once connected, Sasha jumped into the air just in time for a gust of wind to catch his kite and jerk him skyward as the avalanche rushed past beneath him."

"Whew! That must have been a close one," said Grandpa to his grandkids. "Then, being safely carried away from the danger by an air current, Sasha watched from his lofty perch as the huge sliding monster collected and pushed more and more snow, ice, earth, rock and broken trees swiftly down the mountainside below him.

"Sasha didn't consider himself to be a 'wild man,' as the Indigenous People referred to him, but he preferred the name *Sasquatch* to the embarrassing Bigfoot.

"Weeks earlier, Sasha had already decided that when the shaking call signal came, he would take the northern route to Windrail. One of the reasons was the cooler northern temperature on his hairy body. Another was Sasha's fear of humans. He didn't know what they would do to him if he was ever caught and his chances of being seen were considerably less in Canada's north where fewer humans lived.

"Sasha's only encounter with a human had happened late one night when he dashed across an opening in the traffic on Highway 7 near Harrison Mills, BC. Blinded by bright vehicle lights on a moonless night, he hadn't seen the hitchhiker in dark clothing topped by a black cowboy hat and carrying a guitar, on the other side of the highway. The slim hitchhiker was no match for gigantic Sasha when their bodies collided. The man was sent flying and was out cold even before he 'landed in the rhubarb' as they say.

"Sasha knew things would probably not go too well for him if he was found looming over an unconscious person in a roadside ditch. But he couldn't just leave the man in case he was seriously injured. And he definitely wasn't about to try to flag down a passing vehicle for help!

"Without further thought, Sasha grabbed the man with one hand and flipped him over his shoulder. With the other he picked up the guitar and cowboy hat and quickly disappeared into the inky darkness in the direction of the nearby forest.

"The hitchhiker recovered quickly in one of Sasha's temporary camps – a simple clearing in the underbrush of the dense woods with a huge tree growing in the centre. It took a bit longer, though, for the thumb-rider to understand what had just occurred, where he was, how he had gotten there, and especially, who he was now with!

"Both soon established that neither was seriously hurt or in any danger from the other. In short order, Sasha and the stranger, who introduced himself simply as Tom, were recovering, relaxing and somehow communicating. Tom was invited to spend the night.

"The two covered several topics of conversation during the evening. When it came to sports it became quite clear that Sasha was proud of his hop-scotching ability.

"Glancing at Sasha's oversized feet, Tom believed the hairy giant would be too clumsy to perform well and bet his watch that he, Tom, would be better at the game. The challenge was accepted and when the moon broke through the clouds and provided enough light for them to see, the competition began. It would have been hilarious to watch a still-groggy Tom in cowboy boots and a long-footed Sasha as they manoeuvred through the squares of a hop-scotch game. In the end, the nimble-footed *Sasquatch* won.

"When Sasha awoke the next morning, his guest had already left. In payment of the bet, Tom had left his watch dangling from a tree branch in the clearing with a note of thanks for Sasha's caring and hospitality.

Hop-scotch Illustration by
T.L. "Skippy" Drew

"It was about two years later while relaxing at home and listening to country music on his radio that Sasha became aware of the identity of his overnight guest. As the disc jockey announced the next song, *Sasquatch Song*, by Stompin' Tom Connors, Sasha bolted upright. He then listened and laughed as the sound of Tom playing, stomping, and singing the details of a hop-scotch battle came over the air.

"Sasha was honoured that Stompin' Tom had written a *Sasquatch* song after their enjoyable evening together. He also wondered if his guest had been at a disadvantage. Perhaps suffering from a mild concussion caused by his body slam that night, Tom was really the better hop-scotch player. He vowed some day he would return the watch to the only human he knew, had befriended, and trusted. The recent message from Stompin' Tom had given Sasha an opportunity to honour that pledge when he agreed to travel to Windrail to provide protection at a secret meeting of Canadian animals.

"Now, flying high above the snowslide, Sasha realized there would soon be many humans arriving on snowmobiles, ATVs, snowshoes and skis, and in airplanes and helicopters to investigate the avalanche. The debris also made it difficult for him to get to his wilderness home in a hidden cave near Harrison Hot Springs. But he really had no other choice – Sasha had to begin his journey at once. He checked his wrist. The watch he always wore and wanted to return to Stompin' Tom was there. He was ready to go.

"When he had planned for his trip, Sasha knew he might encounter open water, snow and ice along the way. But he also knew his multi-use board, sometimes together with his parachute-style kite, could be used as a snowboard, paddle-board, kiteboard, surfboard and skateboard. He would be able to float, soar, surf, sail, and slide his way over land, muskeg, water, ice and snow. His route would take him north to the top of Canada, then east along the Arctic Ocean's Northwest Passage to the Atlantic Ocean.

67

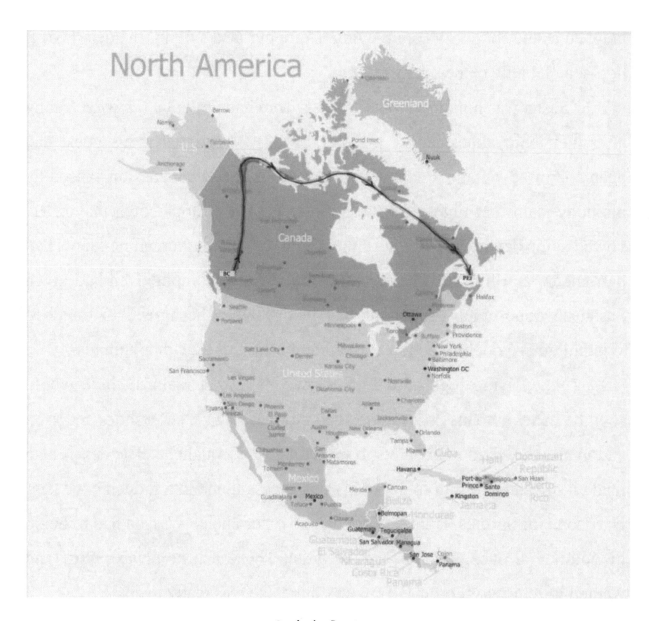

Sasha's Route

"Since there was always plenty of snow on the high tips of the Rocky Mountains even during long, hot summers, Sasha began his trip by soaring and snowboarding north from mountain peak to mountain peak. At one point he was flying high enough in Yukon to see the lights of its capital city, Whitehorse. His bird's-eye view provided him the opportunity to spot mountain goats, elk, a grizzly bear and a cougar. But he did miss seeing a

68

bighorn sheep, the largest wild sheep in North America and the provincial mammal of Alberta. He also managed to glimpse the peak of Mount Logan, Canada's highest mountain, tucked into the southwest corner of Yukon.

Mount Logan

Elk

Cougar

Mountain Goat

Bighorn Sheep

"When Sasha landed near the Mackenzie River in the Northwest Territories, he was standing beside Canada's longest river as it flowed northwest from Great Slave Lake, the deepest lake in North America.

"With Great Slave Lake being the deepest on the continent, I guess Sasha didn't have to worry about there being enough water to float him along the Mackenzie to Tuktoyaktuk," joked Grandpa to his audience.

"At the river, Sasha's snowboard became his paddle-board and, with his kite tucked safely into his backpack, he was able to float down the Mackenzie until the river emptied into the Beaufort Sea at 'Tuk.' From there, Sasha turned toward the east to begin his journey across the top of Canada in the direction of the Atlantic Ocean.

Pingos

"After bouncing off the tops of half a dozen pingos lined up to the east, Sasha set his course toward Iqaluit, the capital city of Canada's newest territory, Nunavut. Iqaluit means 'place of many fish' in the indigenous Inuktitut language. Perhaps because of its low northern temperatures, it's sometimes referred to as Canada's 'coolest' city. How cool is that, eh?

"In his trip across Canada's northern territories, Sasha put his multi-purpose board to many different uses. At times he used it as a snowboard. With the sail attached, he was able to skim atop the wind-swept snow of the frozen tundra, whisked along at breakneck speed by the brisk winds of the prevailing westerlies. In areas of open water he took advantage of huge icebergs – some of them the broken chunks of glacier calving – by flying from tip to tip as he had from peak to peak in the mountains.

"When he managed to gain some height in the air, it seemed as if he could see forever. Occasionally he would spot humans on snowmobiles or ATVs, and even some still using dogs to pull their sleds. One of the teams he saw was just leaving an igloo, a temporary snow-block shelter designed by the Inuit. Teaching its construction to new arrivals to Canada and the North, such as explorers and other newcomer travellers, has saved many lives over

70

the years. An igloo can be built within a couple of hours if you are suddenly caught in a blizzard.

Inuit building an igloo

Dogsled Team

"On a large ice floe he noticed a huge polar bear, the largest bear on earth, and not too far away a seal resting on the ice beside an air hole. He wondered if both bear and humans were after the same prey.

"Sasha's journey didn't bring him close enough to see Yellowknife, the capital city of the Northwest Territories. But what he did see were the incredible displays of the Aurora Borealis - the Northern Lights.

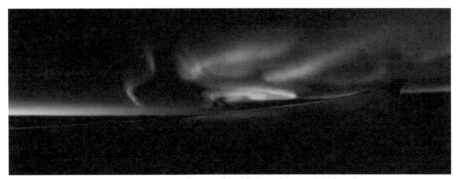
Aurora Borealis (Northern Lights)

"When he reached Baffin Island, Sasha turned in a southerly direction across Québec and Labrador until he reached the Gulf of St. Lawrence. As he passed by Anticosti Island he was careful not to go too close to its dangerous shoreline of rocks and jagged cliffs. Sasha shuddered as he thought about this little known piece of Québec with its horrendous and scary stories of shipwrecks, pirates, people going insane, cannibalism, and starvation. He probably thought to himself that it wasn't much wonder

White-tailed Deer

that an island larger than the province of PEI, is only being shared by a population of less than 250 people and about 150,000 white-tailed deer.

"As he neared the northwest tip of PEI and the beautiful red capes of Kildare, Sasha spotted unusual humps on the calm waters to the east moving toward him. Straining to determine what they were, an instant bolt of excitement passed through him when he recognized them as belonging to his good friend Olga Ogopogo."

It was now time for Grandpa to enlighten his grandchildren on how an *Ogopogo* became involved in the selection of Canada's Big Five animals.

"When Stompin' Tom had contacted Sasha to ask him if he would provide protection and security at *The Secret Meeting Place* at Windrail, Sasha was more than happy to accept the job. Living his life mainly as a landlubber, Sasha also knew he wouldn't be much help to the underwater creatures of the ocean. It was then that Sasha had suggested to Stompin' Tom that perhaps Olga Ogopogo should be considered to assist. She would be more capable in providing safety and security to the marine animals that would be in attendance in the waters below the cape.

"It was now obvious that Olga had accepted Stompin' Tom's request. Sasha also knew that as a professional underwater wrestler, Olga had earned a number of medals and championship belts. He was sure she could handle any challenges that may arise from the problematic *Jipijka'm*. He hoped he could do the same with any threats from *Kukwes*.

"Now, as Sasha hand-paddled his board out to meet and greet his friend, he noticed Stompin' Tom enthusiastically waving them in from the top of the capes at Windrail.

"As the story goes," continued Grandpa, "when Sasha mentioned Olga Ogopogo to Stompin' Tom, he was referring to another well-known mythical creature of the Indigenous People that has become part of Canadian folklore.

"Many, many years ago, people of the Syilx First Nation in British Columbia's Okanagan Valley spoke of seeing a snake-like creature on Okanagan Lake. They called it *N'ha-a-tik* (na-hah-ee-tea) meaning 'sacred spirit of the lake.' They told of how they treated it with respect and avoided the area of the sighting. But in recent years, a report of spotting the *Ogopogo*, as it became known, was usually followed by hordes of people in boats with depth finders, scuba divers with air tanks and masks, and researchers using mini-submarines equipped with lights and underwater cameras. Concern for *Ogopogo's* safety has become such that it has been added to the list of endangered species. Hunting it is not permitted and, if seen, it may be filmed but not captured."

Ogopogo Illustration by Evan D. Maksymchuk

CHAPTER ELEVEN

OLGA OGOPOGO

No one really knows the location of *Ogopogo's* lair," said Grandpa, "but some say it's deep down in a cave beneath Rattlesnake Island on Okanagan Lake."

"Rumour has it that on the day the call came in, Olga Ogopogo was texting with her BFF Kylie and they had just learned that Olga's surname was a palindrome, a word that reads the same backward as forward. That led to a friendly competition to see who could think of the most palindromes.

"Back and forth they texted. Radar, madam, kayak and dad were some of the words they came up with. Then Kylie sent a word that could even be called an upside down double palindrome. She typed 'MOM', then told Olga to turn her phone upside down and of course it became WOW."

"While they LOL'd at their discovery, Olga felt a ripple in the water around her. She knew at once it was the secret signal for which she had been

75

waiting and meant she would have to leave for *The Secret Meeting Place* at once.

"With darting flips of the tip of her tail Olga quickly typed, 'gotta go txt u latr,' before ending the message with her usual signature 'OO' and clicking the 'send' button to Kylie.

"She then swam swiftly upward toward the top of the lake to fill her lungs with air and check for humans, all the while hoping none would be nearby. She would always remember the commotion they made on those rare times when she had been spotted.

"Olga believed it was probably because of the million dollar reward offered for a clear picture of an *Ogopogo* and she also feared that some of those humans might have spear guns as well.

"Fortunately, no humans were in sight when Olga broke through the surface. After taking a few deep breaths of fresh air, she returned home to begin her journey. She had no choice but to leave immediately as she had promised to provide for the safety and security of the water creatures at Windrail.

"It is still unknown – if *Ogopogo* truly exists – how it got into Okanagan Lake in the first place. Some people are of the unproven belief that there could be a natural subterranean river flowing out from the lake to the Pacific Ocean on Canada's west coast.

Traeden questioned, "Underground river, Grandpa?"

"Yes," the elderly man replied, "Who knows what the glaciers that moved through and carved out the Okanagan Valley thousands of years ago created and left behind after they melted away. Now remember, it's just what I have heard and am passing on to you and your sister, but it could also be the reason for *Ogopogo's* disappearances for long periods of time between sightings.

"When this story was passed on to me," continued Grandpa, "I was told that Olga used the subterranean water flow to get out to sea. She relied on her excellent night vision and her knowledge of the route from having travelled through the maze of nature's pipes several times before.

"Even so, when she finally tasted the salty water near a naturally-camouflaged portal somewhere on BC's Sunshine Coast, she felt relieved to be at the end of her claustrophobic swim.

"As Olga emerged from the opening she could already feel the turbulence of the distant Sechelt Rapids at Skookumchuck Narrows through which she would have to swim to reach the Strait of Georgia. 'Skook,' as the rapids is referred to, is one of the great whitewater wonders of the world. It is sometimes claimed to be the fastest tidal rapids in the world.

"Twice daily, when the two tides meet, the difference in water height can be up to three metres, resulting in the formation of swirling whirlpools and churning waves that challenge kayakers and divers from around the globe.

"Skook's violent wave action also attracts many different and unusual types of sea life. This allure may have drawn Olga's ancestors to that area. The result may have been their discovery of a naturally-formed underground passage to Okanagan Lake where they chose to make their home and where

Olga was born.

"When Olga rose to the surface after her long swim from the Okanagan, she was startled by what she saw. There on the rocky coastline, equally alarmed and staring back at her, was a pure white bear. Instinctively, both creatures reacted in the flight mode – Olga by diving underwater, and the bear by disappearing into the brush that lined the shore.

"As soon as she vanished below the surface, Olga came to her senses and realized she had not seen a ghost at all, but had been face to face with a Kermode bear! She had heard about the rare, white-furred but not albino, subspecies of the black bear that was commonly called a Spirit Bear. Although Olga had been momentarily frightened, she was aware of how fortunate she had been to see a Kermode in the wild since they are only found in this part of the world. She wondered what brought it down this far, knowing that their usual habitat is a little farther north in the Great Bear Rain Forest of BC's Pacific Coast.

Kermode Bear
"Spirit Bear"

"When Olga's heartbeat returned to normal and the Skook was free of humans, she swam swiftly and unnoticed through the raging rapids. The rough waters weren't much of a challenge to her excellent swimming ability and before long she was in the Strait of Georgia heading in the direction of BC's capital city, Victoria.

"At the southern end of Vancouver Island, Olga turned in a westerly direction into the Juan de Fuca Strait leading out to the Pacific Ocean. Along the way she resurfaced again to check her bearings and was lucky enough to spot one of the world's few remaining Vancouver Island marmots on the distant rocky shoreline.

"She wondered if the most critically endangered mammal in Canada could be saved. Or would the marmot become another statue of an extinct animal like the huge Tyrannosaurus Rex dinosaur at the world renowned Royal Tyrrell Museum in Drumheller, Alberta?"

Vancouver Island Marmot

Tyrannosaurus Rex
Drumheller, Alberta

"The large number of fossilized dinosaur bones found in Alberta's Badlands between Calgary and the provincial capital of Edmonton, compelled the citizens to erect a statue of the World's Largest Dinosaur. The figure stands so tall it tempts visitors – if they so dare – to climb into the jaws of the huge beast for a grand view of the city of Drumheller.

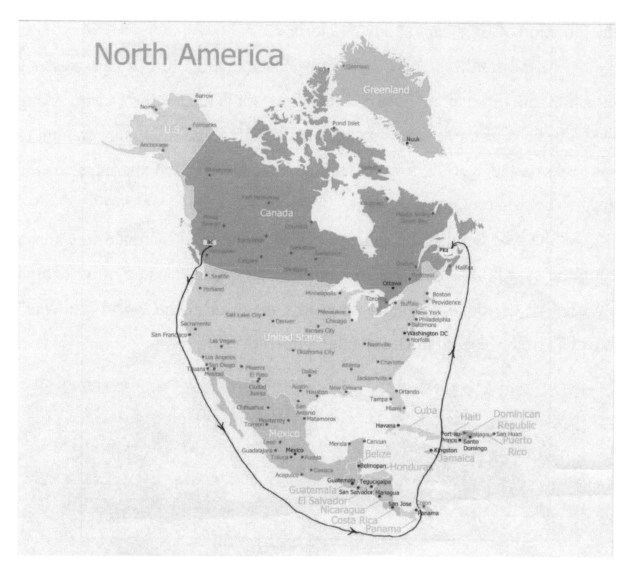

Olga's Route

"Olga continued her westward underwater swim until she was far out from shore, away from any swimmers, surfers and boaters. Only when she felt safe enough did she turn southward. The California Current would help speed her way along the western coast of the United States of America (USA) and Mexico toward the Panama Canal.

"At one time a strip of land called an isthmus joined the two continents of North and South America. With ice and snow covering the top of Canada, in order to get to the opposite side of these continents by sea, ships had to travel a very long way south to Cape Horn. Even today, more times than not, it's a dangerous trip around the tip of South America. It's where the Atlantic and Pacific Oceans collide and create strong currents. The weather is often foggy with gale winds that blow tall waves against a jagged shoreline. Occasionally, even the odd iceberg can be seen bobbing about. It's a mariner's nightmare.

The dangerous seas around Cape Horn

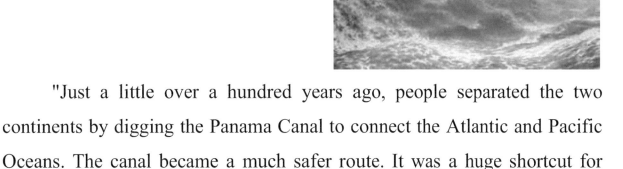

"Just a little over a hundred years ago, people separated the two continents by digging the Panama Canal to connect the Atlantic and Pacific Oceans. The canal became a much safer route. It was a huge shortcut for watercraft from canoes and sailboats to massive cargo and cruise ships.

"Rather than having to dig too deep across the isthmus, engineers designed a system called locks that act as elevators. The locks are huge boxes with doors that can be opened or sealed shut at each end. Water is pumped into or drained out of a lock to raise or lower a ship.

"After entering a lock on one side of the isthmus, a ship is raised to canal water level by water pumped into the lock. The ship is then released to sail the canal to a lock on the other side of the isthmus. The ship is then lowered by draining the water until it's the same height as the opposite ocean.

The Continents of North & South America

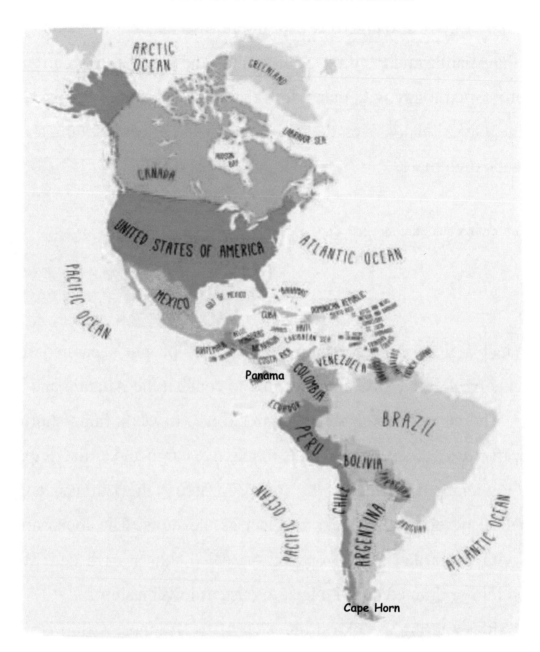

"Originally, two sets of locks were built side by side, but the Panama Canal has recently added a third set. The new locks are deeper, longer, and especially wider because the ships being built today are much larger than those of long ago."

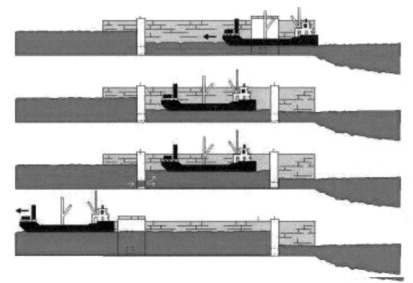

How the locks at the Panama Canal operate
(Cross Section)

Inside a lock

"Although Olga had travelled through the Panama Canal before, this would be her first chance to use the new locks. Having to share a lock with a huge cargo or cruise ship on previous journeys left her with only centimetres of space between the concrete wall of the lock and the steel hull of the ship to squeeze into. More than once she had come close to being crushed by a rocking ship when the lock she was in was being water-filled or drained. This time she was determined to slip into the new larger lock, and hopefully only have to share it with a small ship.

"Even though it was an easy crossing, Olga heaved a sigh of relief when she slipped out of the lock, unhurt and unseen, into the Caribbean Sea.

Electric carts called mules, attached by cables and rolling on rails parallel to the canal, had pulled the large ship in and out of her shared lock. With its engine shut down, she hadn't even had to worry about being shredded to bits by the ship's enormous propeller. Once again she had made the trip through the Panama Canal without being noticed.

"After her cool swim in the Pacific Ocean, Olga felt revived in both body and spirit as she invisibly navigated her way in the warm waters of the sea between the island countries of the Caribbean. The balmy water, hot sun and sandy beaches gave her a homey Okanagan feeling. But that comfort only lasted until she reached the Atlantic Ocean where the water became cooler. Keeping the Florida peninsula on her left, Olga set her course in a direct line to Nova Scotia. Past experience reminded her she was to travel along the east coast of that province and not swim into the Bay of Fundy between New Brunswick and Nova Scotia as she had mistakenly once done.

"A long time ago when she had accidentally entered the Bay of Fundy, Olga was almost trapped between tidal bore river surfers and the drastic changes in depth of the waters she was in. Because of its shape, the bay has two high tides – the highest in the world – and two low tides every day. When the tide comes in, it clashes with the waters of the St. John River flowing out to sea. The rapids, created by the river water being forced to reverse and flow back upstream, is one of the natural wonders of the world.

"On this trip, Olga avoided the entrance to the bay by paying closer attention to familiar landmarks on shore such as the lighthouse at picturesque Peggy's Cove near Halifax, the capital city of Nova Scotia. It was crowded as usual with picture-taking tourists, confirming its reputation as probably the most photographed lighthouse in the world.

Reversing Rapids, Bay of Fundy

Peggy's Cove, Nova Scotia

"Continuing on her way, Olga hoped she would be able to swim through the Strait of Canso, a body of water separating Cape Breton Island from the Nova Scotia mainland. Blocking her way, however, were the Trans Canada Highway and a set of railway tracks atop a two kilometre causeway. Like the natural isthmus at Panama, humans had connected Nova Scotia to Cape Breton Island by hauling in ten million tonnes of rock from a nearby mountain and dumping it into the Strait. They had created an isthmus-like causeway – the deepest in the world – for vehicle and train traffic.

"Also like an isthmus, the human-built causeway blocked the strait and boats had to sail an extra 300 kilometres around Cape Breton Island to get to the other side. So, like the Panama but immensely smaller, a short canal was built across the causeway with a set of locks and a swinging bridge to permit the passage of marine traffic. But Olga was not a boat and the lock was busy with people in vessels of all sizes and shapes lined up to

85

get through. To remain unseen, it was obvious to Olga that she would have to swim all the way around Cape Breton Island to get into the Gulf of St. Lawrence and the Province of PEI on the other side."

Maritime Provinces

"For the most part, Olga's swim paralleled the Cabot Trail, a scenic drive known as one of the best road trips in the world. It was named after explorer John Cabot, an Italian whose real name was Giovanni Caboto. He was sailing on behalf of England in 1497 when he landed on the shore of what is now Atlantic Canada.

John Cabot aka Giovanni Caboto

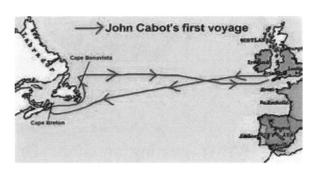

"Once she rounded the northern tip of Cape Breton Island and into the Gulf of St. Lawrence, Olga made a beeline for the northwestern tip of PEI. Always on the lookout for marine creatures she had never before seen, Olga kept watch for a right whale, one of the largest, rarest and most endangered whales. Many years ago, before humans began to try to protect them, they were hunted to near extinction for their meat, bones, blubber and oil. They were easy prey as they stayed close to the coast in search of food and floated when killed. She had heard that one had been sighted near the Bay of Fundy. When none were seen, Olga continued to keep watch in case they were now in the Gulf of St. Lawrence.

Right Whale

"After passing south of Québec's Îles-de-la-Madeleine (Magdalen Islands), she noticed a dark figure kiteboarding toward the same destination from the direction of the Gaspé Peninsula. When both got close enough to the tall red capes of Kildare and each other, Olga immediately recognized her dear friend. It was Sasha Sasquatch! Although Sasha had travelled over the top of the North American continent and Olga around the south, both had arrived at *The Secret Meeting Place* at the very same time."

Bazil the Black-Tailed Prairie Dog Illustration by Evan D. Maksymchuk

CHAPTER TWELVE

BAZIL THE BLACK-TAILED PRAIRIE DOG

It felt like a mild earthquake," began Grandpa with another animal story that easily captured the attention of Traedan and Emma. "The trembling had begun at sunrise in Saskatchewan's Grasslands National Park where Bazil lived with his parents and siblings. Fast asleep two metres underground in his family's burrow, he was awakened by grains of sand that were being shaken loose from the ceiling and tickling his face. At first, Bazil was alarmed, but when he became fully awake he realized what was happening and was no longer afraid. It was the signal he had been waiting for, reminding him he had to leave at once for *The Secret Meeting Place*.

"Bazil was a Black-tailed Prairie Dog. He looked similar to the gophers that are so common throughout Canada's prairie provinces but he was twice their size. He could also be identified by the trademark black tip on the tail of his otherwise brown body.

"Black-tailed prairie animals. They live in draw many human hoping to see and video  dogs are very social family colonies and curiosity seekers their kissing greetings because they closely mimic those of people. The only place in Canada where black-tailed prairie dogs exist is a small area in southwestern Saskatchewan. Sadly, the species is on the Endangered list.

"It usually took Bazil a couple of hours to eat his breakfast of roots and grass, but today he was so excited that he gobbled it down in less than an hour. Soon after eating his fill and kissing his entire family goodbye, Bazil retrieved the black-and-grey-striped railroad cap he had found beside the train tracks several weeks earlier and placed it on his head. Finding it seemed to confirm he had made the right decision in choosing to 'ride the rails' to Windrail.

"Bazil had lived his entire life around the freight trains that were used to shuttle and carry grain from Canada's Prairie Breadbasket to markets around the world. He had also taken enough train rides to become familiar with their routes and timetables and was aware that many carried edible items that dribbled onto the cracks and crevices of grain hopper cars or lay along the tracks. Otherwise wasted, it would be food that he would be able to eat along the way.

"The first train Bazil hopped aboard was a freight that took him to the railroad station in Assiniboia. On the next he continued north on his way to Moose Jaw where he would cross over the CPR tracks and connect with the main line of the Canadian National Railway or the CNR as everyone called it. Depending on his chosen route, Bazil would be switching rides between the two railways. Although the CPR still ran west to Vancouver, BC through Craigellachie where the last spike was driven, it petered out around Montréal in the opposite direction and no longer went all the way east to the Atlantic Provinces. For that, he would have to rely on the CNR, the second transcontinental railway, still serving Canada from sea to sea.

"A loud roar brought him back to reality. Looking up, he realized his train was approaching Moose Jaw near the home of the Royal Canadian Air Force Snowbirds. The noise being made came from the Air Demonstration Squadron's nine Tutor jets returning to their nearby base from practising their formations and manoeuvres. It was a sight to behold and Bazil had the perfect seat!

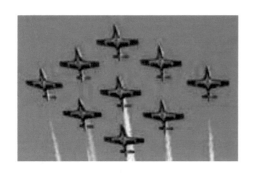 

Motto in Iroquois:
THE HATITEN RONTERIIOS
"Warriors of the Air"

Snowbirds' Squadron Badge
displaying the head of a male
Iroquois Warrior

"The train slowed as it rolled into Moose Jaw, blowing its whistle at street intersections while making a long arc to the right to join the mainline tracks of the CNR leading east. In the short distance through the city, the rail cars crossed the winding Moose Jaw River four times. Now knowing he was on the right track, Bazil relaxed the claws he had crossed earlier for luck and gave a huge sigh of relief. Thinking about the crossings, he wondered if the train had also rumbled over any of the underground tunnels advertised as a sight-seeing venture for tourists.

"Buried deep below the city streets is a series of passageways and secret chambers adjoining the cellars of Moose Jaw's downtown buildings. Rumours have it that they were built by Chinese railroad workers seeking refuge to escape persecution or to hide illegal immigrants. The more popular stories are those of the tunnels serving as a hideout for the infamous American, Al Capone, whenever he went on the lam – which means to run and hide from the law, kids. Apparently the mobster fled to Moose Jaw whenever the G-men – short for Government-men, usually the Federal Bureau of Investigation (FBI) – made his illegal liquor bootlegging business too hot back home in Chicago, USA. To Bazil, thoughts of life underground

brought on an early pang of homesickness.

"As the train rolled east atop its steel-rail road away from Moose Jaw, the time between the clickety-clack, clickety-clack, clickety-clack of its wheels became shorter and shorter. Bazil pumped his paw and gave out a barking yip for 'YES!' It was a sure sign they weren't about to stop and were picking up speed for a dash across the grassy prairie plains. He turned just in time to catch a glimpse of Mac. The tallest moose statue in the world stood overlooking its urban domain from the side of the nearby Trans Canada Highway. Then, with a fifth and final crossing of the Moose Jaw River, Bazil was on his way toward Regina, the capital of Saskatchewan.

Mac the Moose

Pronghorn

"It wasn't long before the locomotive was pulling its cars full steam ahead across the flatlands. Bazil was about to curl up and catch forty winks when he noticed a band of pronghorns running in the field beside him. As they ran, they were slowly edging ahead of his rail car. He knew they were the fastest land mammals in North and South America, but he was surprised to see that they could outrun a fast moving train!

"Many people call them pronghorn antelope, although they aren't antelope at all. In fact, giraffes are their closest relatives. With a top speed of 72 kilometres per hour, a pronghorn can't outrun a cheetah, the fastest land animal in the world over short distances. But they are capable of running at fifty-five kilometres per hour for up to six kilometres, long after the spotted cat would have become winded and abandoned the race.

"Pronghorn may be the second fastest runners but what they have in speed they lack in jumping ability. They can't jump fences and as more and more of those obstacles are built, their range becomes smaller and smaller. Deaths and serious injuries increase along with the number of fences as they get tangled up in their attempts to get under, over or through the wire barriers, especially if the wires are barbed.

"Sitting comfortably atop the fast-moving boxcar and clinging to his railroad cap, Bazil snuggled against the catwalk on top of the hopper car and closed his eyes. He wondered if a pronghorn representative would be running all the way to Windrail and whether it would arrive there before he did.

"As he began to fade, Bazil was jerked from his snooze when a vision of a bloody mangled body of a pronghorn, hanging on a fence, flashed in his mind and startled him to full attention.

"Now fully awake, Bazil noticed a herd of bison off in the distance. Sometimes called Buffalo, the largest land animals on the continent were grazing on a faraway knoll. It brought to mind the stories he had been told of the bison being killed off almost to extinction in North America over a century ago. Many were shot by people from the windows of moving trains just for the sport of it. Others were killed solely for the price of their hides, their edible bodies left to rot under the hot prairie sun, depriving Indigenous People of a prime food source.

"Years ago, as the slaughter went on in some good hunting areas such as the banks of Wascana Creek near Regina, the bleached bones of the bison were piled high. So high, it earned Saskatchewan's capital city its original name of Pile o' Bones.

"Unnecessary killing of bison reduced their number to a critical low, but thankfully, they are now making a comeback as free-roaming animals on the prairie plains of our nation."

Bison Bones

"Bazil changed his mind about the route he would be travelling before the train he was on reached Winnipeg. The capital of Manitoba reminded Bazil of a children's book his mother had read to him when he was just a young chuckling. It was a story inspired by a black bear cub captured by a trapper in White River, Ontario and sold to a soldier passing through by train bound for World War I in Europe. The soldier, a veterinarian on his way to look after the horses being used in the War, named the bear Winnie after his hometown of Winnipeg. He took her by train and ship to England to be his cavalry's mascot. But when the Fort Garry Horse Corps left England to fight in France, it was too dangerous to take Winnie along. She ended up in the London Zoo.

Captain Harry Colebourn & Winnie

"An author in England named A.A. Milne saw Winnie at the zoo and wrote stories about the bear he called *Winnie-the-Pooh* for his grandson. The books became so popular that a statue in honour of Winnie was erected in a park in White River. A chance to see the statue was an opportunity Bazil didn't want to miss, but only CPR trains ran through White River. He would have to switch trains and Winnipeg was probably the best place to do so.

"After passing through Regina and while still in Saskatchewan, Bazil wished he could stop the train in Broadview. Stuffed, mounted and on display inside a museum in that small town was another symbolic figure of World War I. It was Sergeant Bill, a Saskatchewan goat and mascot of the 5th Infantry Battalion of the Canadian Expeditionary Force. A book called *Sergeant Billy,* written by Mireille Messier, tells of how the soldiers managed to sneak Sergeant Bill over to Europe where he saw plenty of action and survived being wounded. Apparently, during his service he saved three soldiers' lives by butting them out of the way just before an enemy shell landed and exploded where they had been standing. Bill warned of enemy approaches and he guarded prisoners. And even though he was court-marshalled for eating the Infantry's paper personnel roll, he returned home a decorated and honoured hero."

Emma shouted excitedly, "Can we get that book to read, Grandpa? Please? Pretty Please?"

"We can try, Emma," answered Grandpa, a bit startled by the outburst.

"We'll get Grandma to check with Amazon on her iPad and maybe even go to the library tomorrow to find out more about it."

Sergeant Bill,
Broadview, Saskatchewan Museum

Then Grandpa carried on with his story.

"There was no stopping the train in Broadview, so Bazil would have to wait for another time. His task now was to plan for a train-change in Winnipeg.

"Both the CPR and CNR have rail yards in Manitoba's largest city and in some places the distance between the tracks of the two railways running parallel to each other is only several metres apart. With a good knowledge of railroads and a keen eye, it wasn't long before Bazil got his chance. It was a perfect opportunity. At about the same time as the cautious slow-moving locomotives began their crossing of the Red River, Bazil noticed the large CP letters on the front of an engine travelling on a nearby track. Once again,

CP Rail train pulling covered grain hopper cars

knowing the alphabet paid off. The letters confirmed it was a CPR train and it was a long one, made up mostly of covered grain hopper cars. He would have plenty of time to run across the rough, grassy land and hop aboard before the tail end car rolled through.

"Looking ahead, Bazil could see that the space between trains would be narrowest on the far side of the Red, so he waited until the CNR car he was on was across that historic river before he began his run. Once aboard the CPR, it didn't take Bazil long to find a secluded and comfortable spot atop a similar car. With his paw still clutching a clump of grass he had snatched during his dash between trains, he settled in for a snack. Relaxed as he munched, he began to hum a Stompin' Tom song while the words passed silently in his mind:

Can ya hear that big eight wheeler
Go clickin' down the rail,
We're on the Flyin' C.P.R.
And believe me she can sail;©

"Bazil was thrilled to think he would now be riding through White River and able to see the Winnie-the-Pooh statue. That alone was exciting, but he was also aware that his trip would now include the Ontario city of Thunder Bay. Just east of that city, he had heard, was a monument honouring a brave, one-legged fellow with an animal name. The young man had tried to run all the way across Canada in support of cancer research. But that dreaded disease itself had stopped Terry Fox where his statue stands today.

"With hopes of seeing the memorial and learning more about the one-legged runner, an amazed but sleepy Bazil began to fade towards dreamland. His final thought before sleep overtook him was that he had just run a few metres between trains on *four* legs and he was pooped. How had Terry run so far across Canada with only one...?"

"It was dawn when Bazil's train approached Thunder Bay. With the number of hopper cars it was pulling, he guessed it would be going down to the waterfront of Lake Superior, the western Canadian end of the St. Lawrence Seaway System. The System was the largest inland waterway in the world. With Thunder Bay Port having the largest storage capacity in North America, the grain from the trains' hopper cars would be unloaded for later pickup and delivery by ship. Freighters sailing the Great Lakes and

St. Lawrence River would load and haul the prairie harvest bounties out to the Atlantic Ocean to customers somewhere in that part of the world."

Grandpa then made a decision. With his water glass empty and his orally overworked parched tongue in dire need of saliva, it was time for a break.

"Can anyone give me the names of the Great Lakes?" he questioned, with a mouth feeling full of cotton balls.

Shouting out their answers, both Traedan and Emma were able to correctly come up with Erie, Ontario, Huron, Michigan and Superior. Emma even managed to add that she knew Superior was the largest freshwater lake in the world just by its name.

"That's very good," said Grandpa. "Both of you continue to amaze me. But I don't think you'll be able to answer my next question."

"All but one of the Great Lakes are partly within Canada. Which one is completely inside the United States?"

"Michigan," replied Traedan confidently. "I remember because it's even named the same as one of the states."

"Well you both certainly earned a break for refreshments," said Grandpa, shaking his head and raising his eyebrows in delightful wonderment. He picked up his drinking glass and headed for the kitchen tap. Grandpa had just downed his glass of water and was sucking on a sour candy to get his salivary glands back in action when Grandma and the kids let him know they were anxious to hear more of his story. And so he went on:

"The train Bazil was on hadn't even come to a full stop before our prairie dog was off and running toward an eastbound freight that was slowly pulling out of the Thunder Bay Port. After clambering aboard, he bounded along the top of the hopper cars toward the diesel locomotive. Bazil wanted to be on the first car when it reached the Terry Fox monument. His aim was to face the rear of the train and pace its speed by 'running on the spot' while the long line of cars passed beneath him. If the choo-choo wasn't travelling faster than he could run, he would be able to stay abreast of the memorial. That would give him an opportunity to study the statue until the last car rumbled along.

"What Bazil learned from the inscription on the statue, and in the days to come, would convince him that Terry Fox was indeed a national hero of Canada and an inspiration and role model to others.

Terry Fox Monument
Thunder Bay, Ontario

"Terry Fox was just a child when his family moved to BC from his birthplace in Winnipeg, Manitoba. He was a good athlete, including distance running, while growing up but was diagnosed with bone cancer at the early age of eighteen. As a result, his right leg had to be amputated. Through dedication and determination, he continued to run using an artificial leg.

"Not many people paid much attention to the one-legged young man when he dipped his runners in the Atlantic Ocean at St. John's, the capital of Newfoundland and Labrador, in April, 1980. Those who asked, learned he was determined to run a marathon a day – just over 42 kilometres – until he reached the Pacific Ocean in a *Marathon of Hope* to raise 'a dollar from every Canadian' for cancer research.

"By the time he reached Ontario, Terry was already becoming a national star, making public appearances and raising money. His increasing fame was not lost to the Ontario Provincial Police (OPP), Canada's second largest deployed police service. The OPP was so in awe of the determined young man, it assigned a full-time escort for his safety along the Trans Canada and secondary highways during his run throughout their province.

"Unfortunately, on the 143rd day of his quest the cancer had spread to Terry's lungs. He was forced to end his run soon after topping an excruciatingly long upward grade near Thunder Bay known as Caver's Hill. Terry told his OPP escorts, having now become good friends, that it was the most difficult hill he had ever encountered. He died nine months later. If the 5,373 kilometre winding route he had travelled – as shown on an Information Board map near Thunder Bay – was stretched into a straight line, Terry would have already covered more than the distance from coast to coast.

Terry, with OPP safety escort battling Caver's Hill

Reproduced with permission of the Ontario Provincial Police

Photo taken by retired OPP Sergeant Ed Linkewich

(Photo appears on Page 31 of Canadian Passports)

"Terry Fox is a national hero of Canada with many buildings, roads, and parks named in his honour as well as his image minted on a one dollar coin. He raised far more than a dollar for each person that made up Canada's population of 23.4 million at the time and many fund-raising *Marathon of Hope* runs continue to be held across Canada each year. He was the youngest person ever to be named a Companion of the Order of Canada and his legacy lives on.

"After literally running out of train at the monument, Bazil turned his attention to White River and wasn't disappointed when the long metal snake he was on slowed through the small township. He was able to get a good look at Winnie-the-Pooh, sitting there on a tree stump eating honey from a pot just like in the book his mother had read to him as a youngster. The memories the statue brought back were so real, Bazil even thought he saw Pooh wave at him, so he waved back just in case.

Winnie-the-Pooh
White River, Ontario

"Bazil could now relax until he reached Sudbury. Once there though, he would have to change trains back onto the CNR to take him all the way through to the Maritimes.

"The train was still quite far from Sudbury when Bazil spotted his first impressive sight. It was the Super Stack. Built by Inco many years ago for that company's nickel mine smelting operation, it reaches 381 metres into the sky, so high it occasionally tickles the bellies of low-flying clouds. It's the tallest chimney in the Western Hemisphere. Bazil thought it was a good thing it wasn't part of somebody's home since Santa Claus would never be able to scramble down the inside let alone find a place on top to park his reindeer and sleigh.

"The chimney was almost never to be. During its construction, just as six men were putting the finishing touches to its top rim, a vicious gale almost blew it over. A tornado had touched down in the nearby town of

105

Lively, then headed toward Sudbury with the new smokestack directly in its path. The workers clung to whatever they could to keep from being blown off their working platform as the chimney swayed to and fro in the wild swirling winds. But the new Super Stack held its ground and stayed upright, the terrified desperate men weren't blown away and no one was killed or injured.

"Next, not too far from the Super Stack, Bazil spotted the Big Nickel, a nine metre replica of a 1951 Canadian five cent piece. It's the world's largest coin.

Super Stack

Big Nickel with Super Stack
in the distance

"As the train noisily rumbled through the city, necessarily blowing its warning whistle before entering any street intersections, Bazil kept his eyes open for a southbound CNR train that would take him to Toronto, Canada's largest city and the capital of Ontario. While doing so, he reflected on the stories and songs of Stompin' Tom Connors, the man because of whom Bazil was now riding the rails to Windrail.

"Of course, one song in particular, *Sudbury Saturday Night*, came to mind. It was the tune that had propelled Stompin' Tom to fame many years ago and Bazil couldn't stop humming it in his squeaky high voice and doing a little jig on his hind feet as the train rolled slowly along:

> Oh, The girls are out to Bingo
> And the boys are gettin' 'stinko';
> We think no more of INCO
> On a Sudbury Saturday Night.
> The glasses, they will tinkle,
> When our eyes begin to twinkle,
> And we think no more of INCO
> On a Sudbury Saturday Night. ©

"When the song first hit the air waves, a few Sudburians were insulted in the belief that Stompin' Tom was mocking them and their blue-collar way of life. Once they realized he was spotlighting their vast and diverse culture by exposing his love of Canada and its hard-working people, it became one of his most famous songs.

"By the time Bazil was leaving Greater Sudbury, he was back on a CNR train enroute to Toronto where he would pass by the CN Tower.

Built by the CNR, it was the tallest free-standing structure in the world at the time of its completion. Today it stands as the ninth, but has been named as one of the Modern Seven Wonders of the World.

CN Tower, Toronto

"Bazil's eastbound train left Toronto to travel the northern shore of Lake Ontario toward Kingston where the waters of the Great Lakes narrow to become the St. Lawrence River. The train engine chugged along the north bank until it reached Montréal. It then crossed over to the south side of the St. Lawrence before continuing easterly toward Québec's provincial capital, Québec City.

Battlefields Park, Québec City
Site of the Battle of The Plains of Abraham (1759)
and the Battle of Sainte-Foy (1760)

"Bazil decided to get some exercise and enjoy the view from the top of the boxcars. As he moved along at a leisurely lope, enjoying the splendour of the St. Lawrence River Valley, he unexpectedly got the fright of his life. While the train was rolling past the Plains of Abraham where the last major battle for Canada was fought between France and England, Bazil was making a jump across the gap between cars. Halfway through his leap, while still in midair, he spotted something that caused all the hairs on his body to stand on end. Sitting comfortably with its back to Bazil and blocking the catwalk ahead, was a creature he had never before seen. Unable to turn around or stop, Bazil was forced into an awkward landing. His sharp claws made a shrill screeching sound as he uselessly tried to dig them into the hard steel walkway to halt his forward slide. Alerted by the commotion, the new traveller leapt to all fours, twisting at the same time to face Bazil.

"Both animals reacted to their primeval instincts as adrenaline pumped through their bodies. Bazil stood his ground, quivering from the sudden surge of the survival hormone rushing through his every muscle. In only a split second he had to decide on which of his two options he should trigger – fight or flee. He had but an instant to assess this evenly-sized opponent in front of him. Its pink nose at the end of a long snout seemingly even pinker between two black eyes and a pale face. Its mouthful of multiple sharp teeth were bared as it slobbered and hissed like a cat. He even noticed the hairless tail at its backside. Lastly, he spied the four short legs attached to feet that appeared firmly planted with no intention of retreating.

"Bazil bravely elected to test his adversary. Ever so cautiously, in hopes of intimidating his foe, he stretched out a front leg as if to take a challenging step forward. He didn't expect what happened next. As soon as he moved, the newcomer collapsed, causing Bazil to recoil in total surprise.

"Transfixed by disbelief, Bazil stared at what now appeared to be a lifeless body laying motionless on its side. As if in death, it's mouth was wide open with lips drawn back to expose froth-covered teeth and a protruding tongue. Then he caught the unmistakable foul odour of rotting flesh, forcing him to snort and step back a couple paces. He was now convinced that the animal lying in front of him had died of fright.

"Confused and not knowing what to do next, Bazil stayed warily crouched on his belly and kept an eye on what he believed to be the dead body of an unknown animal. Then, after a few minutes had passed, he thought he caught sight of a flickering ear. Yes,...there it was again!

"It took some time, but after several minutes, the creature recovered from the third survival option nature had provided that specific animal. Bazil would soon learn that in addition to running or fighting in a life-threatening situation, an opossum will sometimes pretend to be dead or what is aptly called 'play possum' in order to survive.

"By the time both Bazil and Ginnie, as she later introduced herself, were fully recovered from their tumultuous chance encounter, they realized they were on the same mission to *The Secret Meeting Place* and not in any danger from one another. Living in the suburbs of Montréal, and only by coincidence, Ginnie had clambered aboard the same eastbound freight train on which Bazil was riding when he came through the city. They were both travelling to Windrail so they excitedly agreed to continue on together.

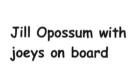
Virginia Opossum

Jill Opossum with joeys on board

"Opossums, commonly called possums, are Canada's only marsupial mammals – animals with a pouch like their Australian kangaroo cousins. That means their babies, called joeys, are not fully developed and only about the size of a bean at birth. When born, joeys must crawl into their mother's pouch where they feed on milk for a couple of months before they are ready to meet the world. When old enough to be out of the pouch but not yet on their own, joeys, sometimes up to a dozen, can be seen getting around by clinging to their mother's back. Bazil laughed at the memory of a nursery rhyme when Ginnie told him that male opossums are called 'jacks' and females 'jills.'

"Due to climate change, opossums appear to be moving further and further north into Canada from the United States. They don't like cold weather so they tend to hug the southern border areas of BC, Ontario and Québec.

"Just before reaching Riviere-du-Loup the train turned south, away from the mighty St. Lawrence River. As they left the longest inland waterway in the world, Ginnie and Bazil were already well acquainted and enjoying the sights and saint names of Québec's quaint towns. Nearing the New Brunswick border, one in particular tickled both of their funny bones when they read the sign that said Saint-Louis-du-Ha! Ha!. Apparently it's the only town in the world with two exclamation marks in its name.

"After crossing the provincial border, but before reaching the capital city of Fredericton, the train veered eastward to Moncton where the railroad ride for the two special stowaway passengers would end.

111

"In many locations across Canada, stretches of railroad lines have been abandoned. The tracks have been removed and the beds molded into recreational trails. When PEI joined Canada as its seventh province in 1873, railroad tracks ran its entire east-west length from tip to tip. Close to a century and a half later, the line went from rail to trail.

"That didn't faze Bazil. He searched the nearby lineup of tractor-trailers for a unit that was being loaded to haul goods from the train station to either Tignish or Alberton in the western end of PEI. From either of those towns it would be an easy jaunt to *The Secret Meeting Place*. He found one quite quickly and he and Ginnie sneaked on board without being seen. The bad news was that the trailer was completely covered and they wouldn't be able to see the Confederation Bridge over Northumberland Strait. They would also miss the beautiful view from anywhere along 'The Link,' as the bridge is commonly called by the locals. Built at the shortest distance between the two provinces, it connects Cape Tormentine, New Brunswick with Borden, PEI, at the Abegweit Passage across the Northumberland Strait."

Grandpa couldn't resist any longer. He paused his story, reached over and picked up his Gibson six-string and began to play and sing another Stompin' Tom song. His little group kept him from singing solo. They all enjoyed the puns and references to the former Indigenous identity of the island, "Garden of the Gulf" and "Cradle on the Waves:"

> While Confederation bridges our nation
> To an island so rich and so rare.

I'll be driving Northumberland
Strait, to that wonderland
Garden that's cradled out there.
And I'll bet there's no bridges
Through high mountain ridges
On land or on sea to compare
With the Confederation that bridges our nation
To Prince Edward Island so fair.©

As he returned his guitar to its cradle, a special wooden stand he had built in his small woodworking shop, Grandpa enlightened his audience to some news he had recently heard.

"During this time of Indigenous Reconciliation, PEI has asked that the name of the bridge be changed to *Epekwitk Crossing*," he said, before getting back to his story.

"Huddled together and well hidden within the merchandise and darkness of the semi-trailer, one of Canada's only marsupials and a rodent were silently rolling along the Trans Canada Highway. It was the last leg of their journey to *The Secret Meeting Place*. When he felt the truck begin to lug its way uphill, smelled the sea, and tasted the salty air that was filtering in through tiny vent slats, Bazil knew they were beginning to climb the marvellous bridge. The semi then levelled off only to climb again near the halfway point of the 12.9 kilometre crossing. It was where the bridge rose to its highest to permit the largest of cruise ships to pass beneath.

"Apparently the upright pillars of the bridge are environmentally friendly to the creatures of the sea and have not made a huge negative impact on the livelihood of the many New Brunswick and PEI lobster fishermen.

Northumberland Strait
Confederation Bridge across the Abegweit Passage

"The bridge opened in 1997 and, on just that one specific historic day, people were allowed to walk to the middle of the bridge and back. Your Grandma was one of those fortunate people to do so."

The kids turned to look at Grandma. She was slowly nodding her head in affirmation as she continued with solitaire on her iPad.

"When completed, the Confederation Bridge became the longest bridge in the world over ice-covered water," continued Grandpa.

Confederation Bridge in Winter

"Disappointed at not having seen the bridge, Bazil made a promise to Ginnie even before they arrived at Tignish. He would find a ride with a better view of and from the link connecting Canada to its smallest province on their return trip home. As a bonus, he told her his extra scenic tour would also include a visit to Shediac, New Brunswick, the lobster capital of the world, to see the largest lobster on earth."

World's Largest Lobster

Red River Renée, B.Eng. on Prairie Schooner I
Illustration by Evan D. Maksymchuk

CHAPTER THIRTEEN

RED RIVER RENÉE, B.Eng.

Red River Renée, as everyone referred to her, was in the class of animals known as rodents. She was also a beaver and preferred to be identified that way. Beavers are Canada's largest rodents. They are hardworking and ambitious and Renée certainly lived up to their reputation of always being 'busy as a beaver.' Today was no exception. On this particular day," said Grandpa, "she was hard at work, carefully weaving the very last tree branch into a dam to block a stream that flowed near a Canadian Heritage – Manitoba's Red River. If she built it properly, a pond would appear in the lush wetland and provide a home for hundreds of different plants and animals, some that were already at risk of becoming extinct. Like other dams built by beavers throughout Canada, hers would filter water, prevent flooding and help in creating a healthier ecosystem. Is it any wonder that beavers are sometimes called environmental engineers?

"Renée was aware that sometimes irresponsible beavers built dams in poor locations that caused land to erode and floods to occur. When that happened and became a nuisance or a danger, humans would dismantle the dam or blow it up with dynamite. Before the problematic dam was destroyed, the beaver at fault would, whenever possible, be humanely trapped. The critter would then be taken to a faraway place to prevent it from rebuilding the blockage. Sometimes beavers would get hurt or even killed during this process. Renée didn't want to be responsible for such damage, injury or death, so she was very conscientious about her work.

"In the centre of her dam Renée built a lodge she alone had designed. She was being extra fussy during the construction since it was to be a new home for her family that included four kits. But just as she was weaving the last branch into place, Renée felt a mild shudder throughout the entire project. Startled, she lost her grip on the final bough and watched as it dropped into the marshy water below.

"As suddenly as they had begun, the vibrations stopped. Renée was quick to understand what had just happened. It was the special signal calling her to *The Secret Meeting Place*. There was no time to spare. She swiftly retrieved the fallen stick and rammed it firmly into place. It would keep the dam and lodge safely interlocked until she returned.

"Before leaving the dam site to ready herself for her trip, Renée examined her latest work. Once satisfied that it met her high standards, she measured and recorded it to be 90 metres long. It wasn't the longest she had ever built and certainly not even close to the record-breaking Wood Buffalo Beaver Dam. Recently discovered, the 850-metre-long beaver dam in northeastern Alberta's Wood Buffalo National Park is the longest in the world. It seems only fitting that it sits entirely within the largest national park in North America and the second largest such park in the entire world."

Since Grandpa had now mentioned the enormous beaver dam, he decided to include the history of its creation in his story.

"Beavers began their covert creation of the lengthy dam in the 1970s," continued Grandpa, "I believe they are still working on it to this day and no one really knows what, if any, specific goal they have in mind. According to stories passed along from generation to generation, one of Renée's kinfolk had been a leading engineer during a phase of its construction. Known to Renée only as Bucky, he had spent most of his working years labouring on the dam until his death at twenty-two, a ripe old age for a beaver.

"Bucky was born near the town of Beaverlodge, Alberta where the residents are environmentally conscious enough to honour the rodents that are so critical to a healthy ecosystem. In tribute, the townspeople built what became the world's largest beaver statue. Many, many years earlier, the local Beaver First Nation had already recognized and respected the importance of the beaver by proudly adopting its name.

"Not in his wildest dreams had Renée's distant relative ever believed he would be working far, far from home on what would become the longest beaver dam in the world. But one day, in a case of mistaken identity, Bucky was trapped in Beaverlodge by a Conservation Officer. He was placed in a cage and loaded onto a float plane bound for Fort Chipewyan, the oldest European settlement in Alberta. Just short of its destination in the northeastern corner of the province, the aircraft touched down on Lake Claire. There, Bucky was released to fend for himself in the marshy wilds of

Wood Buffalo National Park. He was in unfamiliar territory and all on his own."

Beaver First Nation Logo

World's Largest Beaver Statue

Grandpa saw the sadness on the faces of both Traedan and Emma. Misty-eyed Traedan was the first to speak.

"That's a sad story, Grandpa. What did Bucky do to be taken so far away from home?" he questioned.

"Humans, not being very good at identifying one beaver from another, had pointed their individual accusing finger at Bucky," Grandpa replied. "They thought he was the beaver that had created a serious danger to people's lives. They mistakenly believed it was Bucky that had been repeatedly blocking a highway culvert causing roadway washouts dangerous to the travelling public.

"There was no way Bucky could explain it was the vengeful work of an irate beaver that had narrowly escaped with its life from an illegal leg-hold trap. The captured animal had escaped by chewing free its mangled paw that was crushed in the jagged jaws of the steel trap. Since then, the enraged beaver responsible had been on a mission of revenge against humans.

"Within weeks of his banishment, Bucky's expertise was recognized by other beavers in the area. He quickly became the leading engineer of the dam being unknowingly constructed within the park.

"For more than three decades, difficult access to the park and its isolated location kept the existence of the beavers' dam free from human knowledge. However, in 2007, the sharp eye of a researcher, studying satellite imagery through Google Earth, spotted its existence and the secret was out. Apparently it is so large it can be seen from space. Renée hoped if she ever got the opportunity to meet astronaut Colonel Chris Hadfield, the first Canadian to walk in space, she would remember to ask if he had seen that monstrous dam during one of his orbits around the earth.

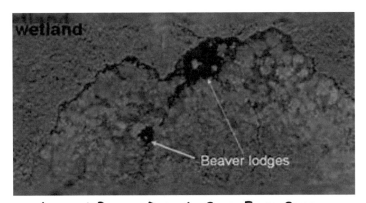 

Longest Beaver Dam As Seen From Space   **Col. Chris Hadfield**

"The park is also home to North America's largest population of wild bison and the natural nesting place of the whooping crane, the largest bird in North America. Above all, Wood Buffalo National Park proudly boasts being a United Nations Educational, Scientific, and Cultural Organization (UNESCO) site.

Whooping Crane

"Red River Renée," said Grandpa, "Was very much aware of the enormous role her species played in Canadian history. Centuries ago, clothing and especially men's hats made of beaver fur, became a fashion rage in Europe. In the land that became Canada, beavers were plentiful and were trapped for their skins.

The pelts were so valuable they were sometimes even used as money instead of cash. But when beavers became fewer and fewer from being over-trapped, the fur-traders and explorers had to travel deeper and deeper into the Canadian wilderness. The search for beaver, in unknown territory that had only been seen by Indigenous People, got explored and mapped along the way. It opened up the land to trappers, fishermen, loggers, prospectors, miners, farmers, ranchers and homesteaders.

"In 1975, Sean O'Sullivan was only twenty years old when he became the youngest person at the time to become a Member of Parliament. Sean realized the substantial contributions made by beavers toward the building of our nation. Even though the image of a beaver is on one side of Canada's 5¢ coin (usually called a nickel), has been on postage stamps, and sits proudly atop every Toronto police officer's hat badge in Canada's largest city, Sean believed they should be more formally recognized. He introduced a Bill to the government and explained how involved beavers were in the creation of our country, its history, and its exploration. It was far more than any other animal. The government agreed, the Beaver Bill was passed, and the beaver became Canada's official animal symbol of sovereignty.

Canadian Nickel

Canada's First
Postage Stamp

Crest Use Courtesy Toronto
Police Services Board

"People call beavers natural engineers and their engineering style so impressed the Canadian Military Engineers that they designed their badge with a beaver as its main symbol.

Canadian Military Engineers Badge

"Renée's parents had always insisted on additional training in their kits' fields of interest so Renée elected to receive higher education in environmental science and huge dam building. What better place to go than Québec where some of the engineers involved in the construction of the hydroelectric dams within that province had also studied and trained. Her choice was École Polytechnique Montréal, even though about a quarter century earlier a young man with a gun had entered the campus and murdered 14 women before committing suicide. Despite the dark wickedness of that terrible event, 'Poly,' as the school is affectionately called, continues to maintain its world-class reputation."

A startled Emma suddenly asked, "Why did that man shoot the women, Grandpa?"

"No one really knows for sure, Emma, but one reason may be anger and hatred from an antiquated belief that women shouldn't get educated for careers that are usually performed by men," explained Grandpa. "Today we believe that all human beings are to be treated as equals, including the right and freedom to choose any career they wish," he confirmed.

"Mom's an engineer!" Emma blurted out defiantly, "And I love building things with my LEGO sets."

Adding additional reassurance, Grandpa confirmed, "Yes, your mother's a mining engineer and we're all very proud of her accomplishments."

"No one was surprised," Grandpa continued on, "when Renée graduated as a Civil Engineer, specializing in dam construction. She was proud to be the first in her family to receive a Bachelor of Engineering (B.Eng.) degree and always included those initials after her name. Presented with an iron ring after graduation at a special 'Ritual of the Calling of an Engineer' ceremony, she was rarely seen without it on the smallest claw of her strongest front paw."

Grandpa then noticed a tiny smile form on his young granddaughter's lips when he encouragingly said, "You go girl! Perhaps someday we'll all be thrilled to see structures designed and built by Emma, B.Eng."

Continuing his beaver tale, Grandpa got back to Canada's national animal.

"Renée had earlier decided to travel to *The Secret Meeting Place* by using Canada's waterways. Beavers have webbed hind feet that help to make them strong swimmers and they can hold their breath underwater for up to about 15 minutes. Their flat leathery tails, usually used for slapping the surface of the water to warn others of danger, are also their steering rudders when swimming. Renée was also intelligent enough to know she couldn't swim the entire distance to Windrail and would need some type of vessel.

"Easily identified by the pink hardhat she always wore, Renée began carving a wooden raft from a suitable log, her large, sharp front buck teeth easily chewing through a tree trunk. The distance she would be travelling wouldn't allow too many rest stops so whenever she had to portage or needed a break from swimming, she could quickly carve a raft and paddles from a tree on shore. She also kept a patriotic flag folded inside her hardhat in case favourable winds called for a sail. The Canadian Maple Leaf with its bright red and white colours would do just fine, blowing her along the surface of a lake or river.

"Food would be everywhere. Whenever she got hungry, Renée only had to chew off a limb from a tree along the way and enjoy its delicious bark. Aspen and cottonwood were her favourites. As she worked on her raft, Renée thought about the route she should travel. Her choice turned out to be the Winnipeg River from its mouth on the lower east side of Lake Winnipeg, southeast to its Lake of the Woods source at the Norman Dam in Kenora. She would be going upstream and have to portage around half a dozen hydroelectric dams but it was the shortest route and was familiar to her.

"It wasn't long before Renée had chipped and chewed her watercraft to perfection. The pole she would use as a mast for the sail fit perfectly into the gnawed notch in the centre of the raft. After dragging what she now referred to as her *Prairie Schooner I* to the edge of the Red River and hopping aboard, she set sail northward, downstream to Lake Winnipeg.

"After leaving Lake Winnipeg's southeastern shore, Renée's upstream trip along the entire length of the Winnipeg River required several portages around human-made concrete dams. Rather than drag her raft around the blockades, she elected to abandon ship and build another on the opposite side of each dam. By the time she reached the last, the Norman Dam in Kenora, she was travelling on *Prairie Schooner VI.* This time, instead of building the seventh, she decided to swim the couple of kilometres to Kenora Bay on Lake of the Woods. There, the docks along the edge of the City of Kenora stretch out like welcoming fingers to the bush planes of summer. It was also near the statue of the town's mascot, Husky the Muskie.

Husky the Muskie

Muskrat

"The sculpture is a replica of a freshwater muskellunge fish usually referred to as a muskie. It's the largest of the pike family, can weigh over 20 kilograms, and challenges fishermen as it prowls the waters of beautiful Lake of the Woods at the top of the food chain.

"As Renée swam silently by Husky's image she snickered as she remembered why and how Kenora got its name. During the early fur-trapping years an abundance of muskrats inhabited the area. There were so many that the settlement came to be known as Rat Portage. Over the years, the number of muskrats declined from over-trapping but when the Maple Leaf Milling Company set up a grinding mill in town, the owners weren't too pleased to see the word 'RAT' printed on their flour sacks. They said it was bad for business.

"There were two other small settlements nearby, so when the Rat Portage townspeople agreed to change the name of their community, they took the KE from nearby Keewatin, NO from not-too-far-away Norman, and the RA from their own town to come up with the unique KENORA. The company was content with the new location address on their bags and the flour sold well.

"A swimming Renée snorted a 'hmmph!,' creating water bubbles with her nose, when she remembered the name-change story. She still fumed when reminded that people seemed proud to wear the fur of a rodent but embarrassed to associate them with food.

"Renée was about to start her log search to build *Prairie Schooner VII* when she heard, then watched, as an incoming bush plane on floats began its landing approach to the invisible officially-designated water runway strip in Safety Bay. The aircraft was close enough for her to recognize it as an Otter.

She had lived in the bush country long enough to be able to identify the 'workhorses of the sky' that seemed to receive names in honour of animals including her own species, the beaver. Other such Canadian-made aircraft are the Caribou, Buffalo and Chipmunk to name a few. It immediately got her thinking, if an Otter can fly, why can't I?

"Abandoning the search for raft wood and slipping underwater, Renée surfaced stealthily beneath the refuelling section of the arrival dock just as two scruffy prospectors she could smell a kilometre away, were deplaning from the now-secured Otter. As she continued to watch the activity around her, she became firmly convinced it would be easy to board the airplane unseen and fly undetected to the plane's next touchdown. In other words, she could become a stowaway. If only she knew the plane's destination....

"Overheard conversations around the dock supplied the answer. As the pilot refueled her plane using a hose connected to a nearby pump, Renée overheard her conversations. The aviator had informally learned the weather conditions between Kenora and Thunder Bay from nearby dock workers and other pilots. It was good news. The Otter's next flight appeared to be to Thunder Bay and Renée was determined there would be a beaver on board.

"Seizing the right moment, Renée darted inside the fuselage and snuggled herself into the farthest back corner of the plane. By the time it was refuelled, the two fortune-hunters in need of a shower from too many days in the bush, were back on board. Renée was already hidden under mounds of reeking unwashed clothing and equipment when the pilot entered the cockpit

Canadian Otter

Canadian Otter

and took her seat. Following the necessary instrument checks and taxiing out to the designated Safety Bay runway for takeoff, it was only a short time before the Otter had the beaver in the air and was droning eastward.

"The noisy landing at Thunder Bay wasn't enough to awaken the distant Sleeping Giant but it certainly snapped Renée out of her deep slumber. As soon as the passenger door opened she made a swift dash out of the plane, bouncing off the wooden dock before disappearing below the surface of Lake Superior. The startled pilot and passengers were left with only a split-second memory of a streak of blurry fur and the sound of a splash as the beaver and the Otter parted company. Neither the pilot nor her stinky passengers could explain or agree on what had just occurred.

Sleeping Giant Island

129

"Surfacing for air after a long underwater swim away from the float plane, Renée was flooded with a feeling of safety, security and comfort. There in the distance, Canada's official colours and the familiar Maple Leaf design caught her eye. It was a feeling that only Canadians returning home to Canada after a lengthy out-of-country absence can share. Proudly wearing the glistening hues and displaying the leaf image was a moored Canadian Coast Guard Ice Breaker and it drew her like a magnet. It would be a safe place to rest, get her bearings and plan her next move, so she headed straight for it.

Canadian Coast Guard Ice Breaker

"During the winter months from December to May, an important part of the many duties of the Canadian Coast Guard (CCG) is to ensure that ports are open and marine traffic can move safely through or around ice-covered waters in the Great Lakes. To do this, the Canadian Coast Guard uses specially-designed or modified ships called ice-breakers. The front of the ship is reinforced so the bow isn't damaged when the ice-breakers push into frozen waters, easily breaking up the ice and making a path for use by other vessels.

"When winters are severely cold and the ice becomes very thick, ice- breaker must rely on its specially-sloped bow so it can ram its front end upward onto the frozen surface and cause the ice to crack and break from the weight of the ship. Not only are ice-breakers used to make paths for other vessels, but they frequently come to the rescue of those ships unfortunate enough to become stuck and frozen solidly in place.

"During the six month summer season, the ice-breakers can be reassigned to other locations, including the Arctic Region. There they assist with duties such as search, rescue and recovery missions, and update training and procedures with Canada's Canadian Rangers.

Canadian Rangers
"Red and Ready"

By patrolling the Arctic, the mere presence of our northern volunteer Rangers reminds the rest of the world that a large North American land mass within the Arctic Circle, including islands and waterways, are part of Canada. And the North Pole is already painted in our official colours!"

"After two days of restful life aboard the Canadian Coast Guard ship, leaving it only long enough to gnaw on some nearby cottonwoods, Renée decided it was time to build *Prairie Schooner VII* and continue on her way. Just as she was about to go ashore, a sudden short shudder shook the entire ship. No, it wasn't another signal from Stompin' Tom. It was a cue to the 19 member crew that the ship was about to depart. Renée had no idea where the ice-breaker was getting ready to go, but from Thunder Bay, anywhere it could sail would take her closer to *The Secret Meeting Place.* She decided to stay aboard, out of sight, and hopefully go unnoticed.

"When the CCG ship pulled out of the Thunder Bay Port, all hands were on deck and too busy to notice the extra passenger silently skulking around the various decks. She was in search of a secluded place from which to comfortably watch the scenery roll by without fear of being caught. By the time the Captain had the ship well under way, Renée was already settled into a perfect location.

"Renée loved all waters – lakes, rivers and streams – while at work building dams and lodges and especially during her leisure time when she was sailing on anything that would float. But her favourite activity was also fraught with danger and Lake Superior was no exception.

"Powerful storms have occurred over the Great Lakes. Those storms begin when cold dry air moves south from northern Canada and crashes with warm moist air coming north from the Gulf of Mexico. Most of them occur in November and many affect Lake Superior, the world's largest freshwater lake by surface area.

"One of the most remembered storms, called the *Witch of November*, happened more than four decades ago. Its vicious hurricane-force winds of over 100 kilometres per hour created ten metre waves, cracking in half the largest freighter on the Great Lakes at the time. The *Edmund Fitzgerald* sank, taking its entire crew of 29 men to their death at the bottom of the lake that sailors refer to as Davy Jones' Locker.

"Today, the legend of the *Edmund Fitzgerald* and the memory of the seamen on board, live on in song by another famous Canadian singer and song-writer, Gordon Lightfoot.

"As the CCG ship cut through the calm waters and the shoreline began to diminish beyond sight, Renée's mind created a picture of the thousands of ships and mariners that lay at the bottom of the Great Lakes.

Edmund Fitzgerald

"She shuddered at the thought that she was probably sailing over some of those corpses at that very moment. Then she gave herself a comforting reminder that it was a calm, sunny summer afternoon and not a dark day in autumn. The *Witch of November* should not be calling.

"The ship she was on passed through the Soo Locks at Sault Ste Marie. The locks accommodate ships as large as freighters bypassing the rapids created by a seven metre drop in the St. Marys River as it carries the water down from Lake Superior into Lake Huron.

"Renée's original plan had been to travel the historic 'water highway to the west,' sometimes called the first Trans-Canada Highway. It was the passage used by explorer Étienne Brûlé when he became the first European to journey west beyond the St. Lawrence River into the Great Lakes area. There he lived for several years with the Huron First Nation, learning their language and studying their culture.

"But there was no way the large ice-breaker she was on would be able to follow Brûlé's historic canoe pathway. Taking that route eastward, as Renée would now have to do, would involve building a raft, paddling the French River and crossing Lake Nipissing to the city of North Bay. From there, several portages would be necessary before she could float leisurely down the Mattawa and Ottawa Rivers to the mighty St. Lawrence near Montréal.

Étienne Brûlé with the Huron First Nation at the Great lakes

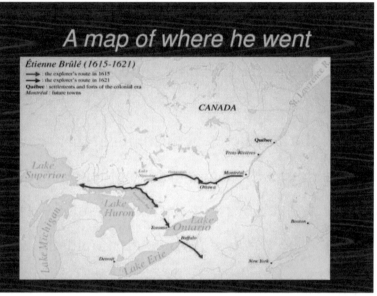

"Then, as if on signal, just as it came abreast of Manitoulin Island – the largest freshwater island in the world – the Coast Guard ship began to turn in a southerly direction. Renée had to make up her mind quickly. Should she abandon ship, swim to shore and continue on her original way, or remain on board the ship that just might take her to the same location by way of the Great Lakes?

"Comfort may have influenced her decision to stay on board, but so did the name on a lifebuoy hanging aboard ship that suddenly caught her eye.

It read, *Captain Molly Kool* and she needed no further prompting. As the ship began its journey toward the lower end of Lake Huron, Renée returned to her comfortable hideaway aboard ship, curled up and fell asleep.

"When Renée spotted the name of the ship she was on," explained Grandpa, "it reminded her of the story of Captain Myrtle 'Molly' Kool, a Canadian from New Brunswick. Eight decades ago as the story goes, Molly became the first woman in North America to be licensed as a ship's captain. She then went on to become the first female Master Mariner in Canada. More recently, she was honoured by having her name attached to the first Canadian icebreaker to bear the name of a female ship's captain. Renée remembered that the *Captain Molly Kool* had been sent to St. John's, the capital of Newfoundland and Labrador, when first put into service. It was now a strong possibility that the vessel was heading back to its home port. If so, it would take its stowaway all the way to the Gulf of St. Lawrence.

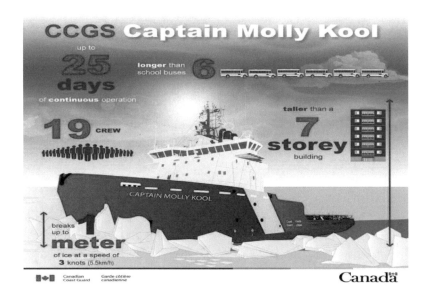

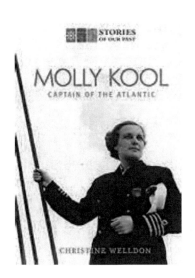

"Renée was still snoozing when the ship reached Tobermory at the tip of the Bruce Peninsula. With her mind faraway in dreamland, she missed seeing the 'flowerpot' rock pillars poking picturesquely out of the water within the SCUBA divers' paradise of Fathom Five National Marine Park.

Flowerpot Island

"The peninsula is also one end of the Niagara Escarpment, a huge land ridge creating a cliff that runs for 725 kilometres and reaches a height well over three hundred metres in places.

"Before she had dozed off for a catnap, Renée hadn't wanted to miss the possibility of perhaps catching a glimpse of a famous rodent living near the lower end of the peninsula. Her internal alarm clock was working well, for she awakened just before the ship reached Wiarton, Ontario, the home of Wiarton Willie. Bluewater Park is home to Canada's most famous white groundhog. On February 2nd – Groundhog Day – of every year, Willie takes a break from hibernation to predict the timing of spring. He emerges from his burrow in the park and if he sees his shadow we can expect six more weeks of winter. If there is no shadow, it will be an early spring. He's known throughout the world and there's even a statue of him within the park."

Statue of Wiarton Willie

"What did Wiarton Willie predict about spring this year, Grandpa? asked Traedan.

"An early one," replied Grandpa, "And as you witnessed, he was correct — as he has been many more times than not over the years."

"Unfortunately, too far out from shore, any chance of seeing Wiarton Willie was impossible.

"Before long the *Captain Molly Kool* was well on its way to the St. Clair River opening that gave the ship access to Lake Erie. Using one of the busiest waterways in the world, the ship sailed down the river, across Lake St. Clair to the Detroit River before entering Lake Erie. Turning east they passed by Middle Island - the southernmost part of Canada - within Point Pelee National Park. What lay ahead was Niagara Falls, one of the seven natural wonders of North America, and Horseshoe Falls, the most powerful waterfall on the entire continent.

Two of the three falls of Niagara Falls

Horseshoe Falls on the Canadian side

"Moving northeasterly along Lake Erie toward Lake Ontario, the *Captain Molly Kool* was sailing atop the Niagara Escarpment. The high ridge had forced four of the Great Lakes to search for a good place to send an enormous flow of water over the brim of the escarpment toward Lake

137

Ontario far below. Always there to assist, Mother Nature obliged and three side-by-side waterfalls were created on the Niagara River, right on the border between the USA and Canada.

"Horseshoe Falls – sometimes called the Canadian Falls – is the widest of the three and drops 52 metres. The smaller two, entirely within the USA, are the American Falls and Bridal Falls. Together, the trio forms what is universally known as Niagara Falls. Water from all five Great Lakes was now free to flow out to the Atlantic Ocean.

"To sail between lakes Ontario and Erie to bypass the falls, ships must be raised or lowered onto or off of the escarpment. In order to do so, the *Captain Molly Kool* pointed its prow northward into the opening of the Welland Canal, built especially for that purpose.

Welland Canal

"The ship was lowered 100 metres through eight locks along the 45 kilometre distance between lakes. As she travelled, Renée listened to the faraway murmur of the falls and gazed at the misty cloud bubble it produced on the distant horizon. Although she wouldn't get a close-up view of the falls, it was exciting to be as close as she was. But Renée was also saddened when she remembered the story of the greedy inhumane actions on the part of humans that led to the first known non-accidental deaths of animals by way of the falls.

"Just about two hundred years ago, three local hotel owners decided they could make money by drawing tourists to town to watch a boatload of animals plunge over the falls. Back then, animals weren't protected from cruelty as they are today and apparently no one protested enough to stop the event. The businessmen advertised the spectacle as a 'pirate ship filled with ferocious beasts' but it turned out to actually be a dilapidated, leaky, condemned schooner named *The Michigan* carrying a buffalo, two small bears, two raccoons, a dog, two foxes, sixteen geese and an eagle. Unbelievably, about ten thousand people showed up to watch.

"At the advertised hour, *The Michigan*, with its doomed cargo of animals tied or caged aboard, was pointed downstream and set afloat above Horseshoe Falls. Immediately caught by the strong current, the vessel was jerked into the rapids with such ferocity the hull was torn open. Somehow the two little bears managed to escape and survived by swimming to nearby Goat Island. All of the other animals were carried to the brink of the falls and sent hurling down to the rocks and swirling waters below. Only one lone goose survived."

Wiping away a tear with her upper arm, Emma blurted out, "Have any people ever gone over the falls, Grandpa?"

"Yes, and some have even lived to tell about it," he replied. "The first was a widowed schoolteacher about the same age as your Grandma and desperate for money. She believed she could become rich and famous by floating over the falls in a barrel. She survived with only a small cut to her scalp but never became rich."

Annie Edson Taylor

(First Over Falls in a Barrel)

"The youngest to survive," continued Grandpa, "was seven-year-old Roger Woodward. He was swept over Horseshoe Falls when the small boat he was in was swamped by the rapids. The lifejacket he was wearing was his only protection but he was fortunate enough to be spotted floating unhurt and was picked up by the Maid of the Mist tour boat at the bottom of the falls."

Grandpa ended up by saying, "Thankfully, such barbaric animal abuses and intentional daredevil acts are illegal today."

"Turning in an easterly direction after leaving the Welland Canal, the *Captain Molly Kool* plied its way along the entire length of Lake Ontario to enter the St. Lawrence River at Kingston, the hometown of Canada's first Prime Minster, John A. Macdonald.

John A. Macdonald

"At the mouth of the St. Lawrence River, Renée couldn't believe her good fortune when the *Captain Molly Kool* pulled into the seasonal Canadian Coast Guard Station at Rivière-au-Renard on the nose of Québec's Gaspé Peninsula. As soon as an opportunity arose, she quickly and silently disembarked and made a dash toward the nearest copse of trees.

"After munching on a few branches to satisfy her hunger, our favourite beaver made her way along the shore until she found a large forested area safe and secluded enough to finally build *Prairie Schooner VII*. During the construction Renée was extremely careful not to disturb or injure any Maritime Ringlet butterflies. The endangered species is extremely rare and can only be found in the Gaspé Peninsula and northern New Brunswick.

Maritime Ringlet Butterfly

"The final water craft Red River Renée, B.Eng. constructed on her journey was a raft worthy of her qualifications. She sat proudly on deck, her strongest front paw tightly grasping a moosewood maple spar. Attached, serving as a sail and billowing in the wind, was her red-and-white maple-leaf flag. She had set a southern course across Chaleur Bay toward PEI's North Cape lighthouse and the *Secret Meeting Place*."

CHAPTER FOURTEEN

UNINVITED HUMAN-EATERS

Bad Billy the Bootlegger woke up to a clear morning sky and a weather forecast that promised sunshine all day long. It was the first day of July – Canada Day. That usually meant a large number of Islanders and tourists 'from away' would be flocking to the local beaches to celebrate the popular national holiday. It had always been one of the best days of the year for Billy's unlawful business of selling moonshine alcohol he distilled in the basement of his home. This holiday would be a bit more interesting. He had recently added cannabis products to his list of illegal items for sale. He was anxious to see how much money people were willing to part with for the added goods that could alter their minds, ruin their bodies and put their lives at risk.

"Bad Billy lived in a ramshackled seaside shanty near Tignish Shore. His self-established sales empire began from his home and took in all the beaches and parks south to Alberton. The only stretch between those two locations usually free of beach-going customers, was the long rocky shoreline along Kildare Capes, *The Secret Meeting Place.*

"The passing years had not been kind to Billy. Perhaps it was his eager desire to sample his wares that made him look old for his age. Had too many toasts made with a sip o' the 'shine eroded his memory and stripped him of common sense? No one could say 'fer shore.'

"After making his way down the path to his rickety dock, he bailed out the water that had seeped into the leaky wooden dory tied there since yesterday. Later, following a few trips to and from his house, Billy had the boat loaded with his black market sales items. Next, with more tugs than normally required on the starter cord – mingled with a fair number of cuss words – he managed to bring his old outboard motor coughing and sputtering to life.

"It was not until then that Billy remembered he had not yet brought down some of the required boating safety items, including his lifejacket. Fearing the clattering, difficult-to-start outboard motor might stall if left unattended, and with an expectation of calm seas on a beautiful day, he foolishly decided to take a chance. Despite living on the seashore of an island, Billy had never learned to swim. Still, he left all life-saving gear behind, even though it meant breaking the law and putting himself in danger.

"In order to get to the long stretch of beach he wanted to visit first, Billy would have to sail along the usually deserted shoreline of Kildare Capes. Unknown to him that morning, much of the waters below the capes would be occupied by marine animals attending *The Secret Meeting Place.*

"Billy was still far off in the distance when Olga Ogopogo, in charge of the safety of the underwater attendees, spotted his approach and instantly realized he was travelling too close to shore for everyone's safety.

"Mumbling to herself that no one would be getting hurt on her watch, Olga quickly dove underwater and swam swiftly out to meet Billy head-on.

"Swimming just below the surface, directly in Billy's line of travel toward her, Olga curled and twisted her body enough to expose her many dorsal fins above the water. She hoped it would give the appearance of a shiver of sharks and cause Billy to go around by steering his dory much farther out from shore.

"But a lifetime by the sea and possibly some numbness of his mind produced little reaction to the sight of 'shark fins' from Billy. Unconcerned, he continued buzzing along on course and it was Olga who had to dive deeper to avoid being sliced up by the blades of the passing outboard motor propeller. In order to protect the marine animals gathering in the waters at the foot of Kildare Capes, Olga was forced to do what she had never done before – intentionally expose herself to a human being.

"Completely underwater, Olga turned and easily caught up to the boat, swam on past it and again waited for Billy's approach. Once he got close enough, she reared upward and did a full-bodied breach. This time, the sudden appearance of a huge serpent-like creature was not ignored. Shocked and horrified at the terrifying sight of a two-horned head of a horse bursting out of the sea, Billy unintentionally jerked the steering arm of the outboard motor. His reflex action forced the boat to make the tightest u-turn ever in its long history. Centrifugal force caused everything inside the boat to fly out and into the water, including Billy. The derelict dory didn't capsize, but the out-dated outboard gave up the ghost. Seconds after hitting the water without a life preserver, surrounded by a flotilla of his illegal products, a dazed Billy began to sink.

"Unhurt, conscious but in shock, Billy didn't struggle when Olga picked him up from the water by her tail and lifted him into his boat. Neither did he speak. White as a spook, he sat frozen to the plank seat. Mouth agape, Billy stared straight ahead through wide unseeing eyes while Olga towed the old dory a far distance in the direction from which he had come. After pushing the boat into a secluded cove on shore, she quickly turned and disappeared back into the sea.

"Billy recovered from the shock and somehow made his way home, but from that day on he never sold another bottle of rotgut home brew or any type of drug. He even turned his life around and stopped using what he once used to sell.

"Not long after his encounter with Olga, Billy gave up trying to convince anyone who would even listen about his brush with a 'sea monster.' Just another old sailor's yarn, they would say. They just didn't believe him.

"When Olga returned to the undersea area of *The Secret Meeting Place*, she couldn't help but notice the large narwhal whale within the gathering group. Her attention was mainly focused on the two-metre-long spiral tusk protruding from the upper jaw of this recent arrival from Baffin Island. It confirmed why those Arctic water dwellers were sometimes called the unicorns of the sea."

"A sudden kerfuffle drew Olga's attention. Seemingly out of nowhere, another tusk-bearing creature had appeared within the crowd and was now face-to-face – or in this case tusk-to-tusk – with the narwhal.

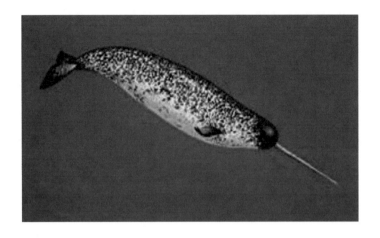

Narwhal Whale
(Unicorn of the Sea)

"The stranger's tusk was also spiral, about the same length as that of the narwhal, but of two colours. It lived underwater and had a body similar in size and shape to Olga, except that its head was very ugly.

"Olga realized at once that the newcomer matched Elder Mathilda's description of the *Jipijka'm* of the Mi'kmaq spirit world. The one with a reputation of being nasty and rumoured to eat humans. The *Jipijka'm's* unpleasant personality didn't win it any friends among the sea animals and it quickly came to realize it would be the underdog in any confrontation with others. It also learned from the other animals that Olga was a trophy-winning underwater wrestler back home in the Okanagan Valley and the narwhal was an expert dueller with its tusk.

"When it became aware that no humans would be in or on the water at the gathering, the *Jipijka'm* seemed to lose interest and swam away. It was never seen again. Just to be on the safe side though, Olga cautioned Stompin' Tom and Elder Mathilda not to go swimming or even too near the sea."

Not expecting an answer, but wishing to serve his grandchildren some food for thought, Grandpa asked Traedan and Emma, "Could it be that Olga had not only saved Bad Billy from drowning, but also from the unicorn sea serpent?"

Without waiting for a reply, Grandpa continued on:

Jipijka'm (Unicorn Serpent) Illustration by Rylan Maksymchuk

"Meanwhile," he said, "in the large open meadow on top of the cape, Stompin' Tom and Elder Mathilda were busy preparing the area around the large flat-topped rock for the upcoming meeting. Both were pleased with the large number of animals arriving steadily and in plenty of time before the meeting began. The only two humans wondered if the sounds of the many different grunts, gurgles and sputters being made by the animals were stories being shared of happenings during their travel from wherever they had come. Elder Mathilda confessed to Stompin' Tom that she thought she may be feeling somewhat the same as Noah had when the animals were boarding his Ark.

"Stompin' Tom checked the wristwatch on his left arm, the same one he had left hanging on the tree for Sasha in payment of his loss over their friendly hop-scotch game. Sasha had returned it to him and insisted on a future rematch when neither of them was possibly suffering from a concussion. Both agreed, knowing full well it was just an excuse to get together again sometime.

"When it got closer to the time to begin the meeting, and without warning, a big dark cloud blocked the sun. It was enough to cause the entire area to turn murky. Instant reaction from the land animals atop the cape was to scatter and skirmish for a nearby hiding place and become completely silent.

"As everyone strained their eyes in a hushed search of the gloom, a gigantic brown figure was glimpsed moving among the tall grass and brush, stealthily making its way toward Stompin' Tom and Mathilda. None of the animals dared to move. Even they had never seen anything like it before.

"Ever so slowly, completely ignoring the animals, the enormous creature got closer and closer to the two people standing side-by-side.

"Stompin' Tom and Elder Mathilda stared in disbelief at what was approaching them. Saliva drooled from the huge jaws of an enormous bear- shaped head perched on top of a hairy body. Both of its individually-controlled eyes emitted a bright yellow rod of laser light. Each eye beam appeared to be searching until it fell and locked onto one of the humans. Once struck, Stompin' Tom and Elder Mathilda were frozen in place. Unable to move, they could only watch in terror as the intruder came nearer with each of its giant footsteps. It was *Kukwes*, the human-eating ogre of Mi'kmaq lore and it had just fixed its gaze onto the only two people around.

"But suddenly he was there — leaping out of nowhere — stepping in front of the monster's path and blocking its harmful jaundiced rays. It was Sasha!... and he was immune to the paralyzing power of the *Kukwes'* yellow light. By jumping in front of Stompin' Tom and Mathilda, the laser beams from the evil boogeyman simply bounced off Sasha's rough furry chest. Though feeling somewhat dazed, once the light was off their bodies, Elder Mathilda and Stompin' Tom were quick to recover and free to move about once more.

"As soon as the *Kukwes* realized what had just happened, the yellow beams and black cloud disappeared. Daylight appeared bright and clear once more. Now aware that its paralyzing laser rods were useless against a *Sasquatch*, the cowardly but quick-minded *Kukwes* thought up a reason to be at *The Secret Meeting Place*. It said it had heard Sasha's favourite sport was kiteboarding and wished to challenge him to a competition at the Magdalen

Islands, a location where the sport was popular but difficult to perform.

"Sasha was not at all convinced that it hadn't been dinner on the *Kukwes'* mind. But not one to back down from a reasonable challenge, he accepted. Going to the Magdalen Islands in the middle of the Gulf of St. Lawrence with the *Kukwes* would keep the beast under his watchful eye and away from everyone at the gathering. It would be a win-win situation."

Kukwes Illustration by Evan D. Maksymchuk

Grandpa went on to describe the Magdalen Islands for his grandkids.

"The Magdalens are very challenging," he said, "A bit dangerous but a popular place for experienced kiteboarders. The islands are well known among avid kiteboarders and windsurfers for the presence of strong currents and gusty south winds. The ideal conditions at Sandy Hook Point are especially attractive to lovers of the sport and even prompted the hosting of the Canadian National Windsurfing Championships there one year," he told them.

"At Windrail, the two giant creatures looked weird after donning their gear, complete with board, kite, helmet and harness. Like aliens from another planet, they ambled to the edge of the highest point of the steep, rocky cape and stood waiting for a strong enough gust of wind to lift them upward and eastward over the Gulf of St. Lawrence. They didn't have long to wait. Just at that moment *Wuchowsen* had arrived to assist the little wind-maker, Noisy Nick. The wind bird was only too happy to take the time to loft the two challengers on their way to decide whether a *Kukwes* or *Sasquatch* is the better kiteboarder.

"A few flaps of *Wuchowsen's* wings caused the kites to swell, dragging and jerking Sasha and the *Kukwess* off the crag. Before long they were soaring upwards into the blue yonder. Within minutes they became two tiny specks in the distant horizon, on their way to join in on the extreme water sports at the Québec islands halfway to Newfoundland and Labrador.

Wind and Water Sports at Magdalen Islands

CHAPTER FIFTEEN

WELCOMED VISITORS

Elder Mathilda had just completed the smudging ceremony and Stompin' Tom was almost ready to begin the special song he had written for Canada Day when a commotion drew them to the edge of the cape. In the distance they could see the heads of two swimmers coming toward them, both with similar horse features. As they got nearer, one was recognized as Olga Ogopogo and she appeared to be guiding the other that looked like a pony. It turned out to be one of the small horses from Sable Island far off the coast of Nova Scotia.

"For many years the Sable Island ponies, the only permanent residents of that Nova Scotian island, had been isolated and unknown to Canadians. No one knows for sure how the original horses arrived on that 40 kilometre strip of land shaped like the smile on a happy emoji. The most common belief is that they swam from a wrecked ship since the barren windy island is surrounded by dangerous underwater sandbars and has claimed hundreds of ships and lives over the years. But despite the island being referred to as the 'Graveyard of the Atlantic,' a more recent belief – and perhaps the most likely – is that the horses were dropped off there as wartime booty. They may have been placed there, for later retrieval, by British seamen during the Great Expulsion of French Acadians from Nova Scotia in the mid-1700s.

153

"One hundred and seventy-five kilometres away, the closest land to Sable Island is Nova Scotia and it is part of that province. It has also become a National Park in an effort to protect its uniqueness and the official provincial animals of Nova Scotia.

Sable Island Ponies

"Olga introduced the newcomer she had spotted out to sea and escorted to shore, as Colter. He explained he was aware that a local Irish moss-raking horse was representing all horses in Canada at the Big Five decision gathering. He went on to say he just wanted to be sure the horses on Sable Island would not be overlooked during discussions. A cheer went up and he was welcomed by everyone. Colter's arrival would be in time for the Canada Day song at precisely 12:00 noon, Atlantic Daylight Time (ADT)."

Grandpa went on to describe the scene at *The Secret Meeting Place* at Windrail. He began by telling his grandchildren that when the clock struck noon, the crowd of various animals atop the cape, in the sea below and in the sky above, would become as hushed as a classroom during a written exam.

"A southern breeze was blowing when Stompin' Tom gently placed his stompin' board on top of the flat rock. He went over to Noisy Nick, flipped its switch and waited until the blades of the wind-maker were turning smoothly at top speed. Satisfied, he glanced skyward where he spotted a speck in the far-above heavens. He knew it was *Wuchowsen*, waiting to encourage the winds of song and sound.

"Excited and full of energy as always, Stompin' Tom sprang up onto the rock, adjusted the position of his stompin' board, strummed his guitar to check its tone in the chord of C and took a sip of H_2O."

"That's water!" cried out the grandkids in unison, sensing the question was about to be asked.

"Yep," said Grandpa. "Stompin' Tom was now good to go. Ready to strum, sing and stomp. At precisely noon the animals underwater, in the air and on land now became very silent. The only sound was the soft whirring of fan blades coming from Noisy Nick.

"As Stompin' Tom began to play and sing the song he wrote especially for Canada's birthday…."

But Grandpa never finished his sentence. Instead, he reached for his guitar and launched into a performance of his own. His family enthusiastically joined in and they sang the entire song together beginning with the chorus:

> O CANADA: Standing tall together.
> We raise our hands and hail our flag,
> The Maple Leaf Forever.
>
> It's Canada Day, up Canada Way,
> On the first day of July;
> And we're shoutin' "Hurray" up Canada Way,

When the Maple Leaf flies high.
When silver jets, from east to west,
Go streaming through our sky,
We'll be shoutin' Hurray! up Canada Way,
When the great parade goes by.

It's Canada Day, up Canada Way,
On the coast of Labrador;
And we're shoutin' Hurray! up Canada Way,
On the wide Pacific shore.
People everywhere have a song to share
On Canada's Holiday.
From Pelee Island in the sunny south,
To the North Pole, far away.

It's Canada Day, up Canada Way,
When the long cold winter's done;
And we're shoutin' Hurray! up Canada Way,
For the great days yet to come.
Where maple trees grow maple leaves
When the northern sun is high;
We're Canadians and we're born again
On the first day of July.

It's Canada Day, up Canada Way,
From the Lakes to the Prairies wide;
And we're shoutin' Hurray! up Canada Way,
On the St. Lawrence River side.
People everywhere have a song to share
On Canada's Holiday.
From Pelee Island in the sunny south
To the North Pole far away.©

"The Snowbirds," puffed the old man, all out of breath at the end

of the song, "on their way to perform in Charlottetown, thundered low

156

overhead when Stompin' Tom was partway through his ballad. That manoeuvre added even more powerful wave vibrations already being created by his famous stomping boot."

Having now caught his breath, Grandpa described unexpected happenings that occurred during the singing of the song and the flyover by the Warriors of the Air.

"The unusual tremors caught the attention and curiosity of colourful Chris Codfish en route to Alberton from the Grand Banks of Newfoundland. Passing through to participate with supporters and members of the LGBTQ2S+ Community at a Pride Parade in Alberton, Chris' temptation to join in and sing in celebration of Canada's birthday was welcomed and supported by those in the sea below the cape.

Chris Codfish

Lester Lobster "Lester Lobster also felt the rhythm of the music at his lobster bed not far off shore. A music lover, he took little time in grabbing his guitar and swimming closer to the sound. Flipping his tail in time to the beat, he kept himself upright on the surface of the sea while plucking at the strings. From many hours of practice, Lester easily matched and slipped the twangy tones of his guitar into Stompin' Tom's song at precisely the right time and place.

157

Lester was pleased to see he was properly adding to the tempo when he got the acknowledging sign — that only guitar players know — from the singer on the rock."

"Secret sign?" interrupted a suddenly very curious Traedan. "What's the guitar players' sign, Grandpa? Do you know it? Do you, Grandpa? Huh?"

"Yes I do," answered Grandpa. "but I can only show you if you learn to play the guitar."

"Awww, shucks," said Traedan. "But I really do want to learn. Will you help me?"

"Of course," promised Grandpa, "Of course I will."

"The only other incident that I'm aware of," said Grandpa, "occurred just as the Snowbirds flew over the Town of Tignish. This one could be classed as collateral damage.

"Not unlike Stompin' Tom's famous *Hockey Song*, the score in the last few seconds of a hockey game being played down at the old Tignish Centennial Arena was tied 1-1. It was a Canada Day exhibition game, a challenge between the Tignish Aces of the PEI Junior C Hockey League and members of the HAB Club from the nearby village of St. Louis. Plucked from within its small population, the recreational team of hockey enthusiasts reflected a good cross section of the potato-producing village people."

Traedan rudely piped in again, "What's HAB mean, Grandpa?"

"What does HAB mean?" Grandpa responded, "Hockey And Ball according to the players, Traedan, but if you questioned any of the locals they will probably say Have A Beer," joked Grandpa, causing everyone to laugh.

"Anybody you asked said the top-of-their-league Tignish Aces were a cinch to win, especially with the lightning reflexes of their goalie 'Krusher' Kelvin between the pipes. They said he could block everything coming his way. Such was his reputation that if he didn't have to wear a face mask, he could catch the puck by his teeth, crush it between his jaws and spit it out in pieces.

"But the HAB Club also had an ace up their sleeve. He was known as Reggie Reynard and was as sly and foxy as his surname. You see, Reggie was really a silver fox, but in his mind he believed he was a human being and no one could convince him otherwise. He was a descendant of a male ancestor who, together with a vixen, had escaped from a fox farm on Cherry Island where certain death had awaited them many, many years ago.

"Cherry Island – now called Oulton Island – just off the shore of Alberton, is where silver foxes were first in the world to be bred and raised successfully in captivity. Expensive silver fox furs quickly became the newest fashion craze and extremely popular among royalty, nobility and the rich and famous throughout the world. Fox-farming turned into a huge industry in PEI and made many an Islander extremely rich. In appreciation of the silver foxes' contribution to the economic boom, the province of PEI redesigned its official coat-of-arms to prominently and gratefully, include them on its crest.

PEI Coat-of-arms

Silver Fox

"Reggie Reynard was born in St. Louis, PEI, in the wooded swamp behind the F.J. Shea & Sons general store that everyone calls Frankie's. It was where the fugitive family had always lived and hid in plain sight, not too far from the now-abandoned fox farm. They had even brazenly chosen the surname Reynard, which is another word for fox. The tactic seemingly left the silver fox family to go about their lives unnoticed and their hides safe from becoming fashionable garments for the wealthy.

"Reggie loved hockey and every chance he got he practiced skating and stickhandling. Alone on the frozen slough ponds behind Frankie's, he would dart and leap around, between and over the bunches of bulrushes. One winter day while practicing, Reggie was spotted and watched by a HAB Club member. His amazing performance quickly got him an opportunity to play in a local pickup hockey game and the rest, as they say, is history.

"On the ice, he was like a furry Gretzky. He always seemed to know where the puck was going to be and could zigzag around opposing players like a terrified rabbit being chased by a hungry bobcat. Perhaps a bit exaggerated, they said he could shoot the puck faster than a bullet, then dash

160

and catch up to it on a glinting blur of his steel blades.

"Back at the hockey game in Tignish, expecting the buzzer ending the game to sound at any second, the HAB Club superstar was carrying the puck down the ice at breakneck speed. After picking up a pass, Reggie had deked out the last player between himself and the net. He was now all on his own. It was a one-on-one situation between him and the Tignish Aces' Krusher Kelvin, the top goalie in their league.

"Reggie knew he would already be a few minutes late for the gathering at Windrail. He was the one that had been appointed to represent all foxes in Canada and knew they were counting on him to be there to vote for Canada's Big Five. If the game ended in a tie and went into overtime, he would have to make the decision whether to miss the rest of the game or miss the voting. He neither wanted to abandon his HAB Club buddies nor let the fox species down. He had to be there. He had to score a goal in order to win the hockey game before the third period ended, then rush to get to *The Secret Meeting Place* on time.

"It's amazing how many thoughts can pass through someone's mind in a split second," continued Grandpa to his grandkids. "When the Snowbirds buzzed low over the arena, the rumbling sound they created caused the old building to shake and tremble. But Reggie's attention was attracted to an opening above the slight but taunting wriggle of Krusher's gloved hand. It could have been an old trick used by goalies to catch the eye of the shooter and bring the puck right into their catch glove. But it could also have been a genuine challenge by the goal keeper. As Reggie continued stickhandling at

161

full speed, he wondered if Krusher was playing him for a sucker. Then, by reflex and coincidence, the following things happened simultaneously:

"Reggie began a snap shot, aiming to put the puck top shelf just above the goalie's taunting glove – where Grandma keeps the peanut butter as the hockey commentators would often say; Krusher's gloved hand began moving upward to cover the attractive open hole into the net where he was tempting and daring Reggie to send the puck; pressurized artificial ice pipes beneath Reggie's skates began to crack; and, the buzzer ending the game clicked to begin its final sound.

"All the vibrations were just too much stress for the antiquated pipes full of compressed gas used in making artificial ice. At the same time as Reggie's stick connected with the puck in the final shot of the third period, the shivering metal tubes, weakened over use and time, burst open.

"The explosive pressure thrust a large chunk of ice, carrying Reggie along with it, upward between the rafters and through a new hole in the curled-back tin of the arena's roof. While hurtling through the air, Reggie's frozen flying saucer passed overland directly toward the shore of Kildare Capes. It splashed down beside an ice floe upon which a huge white bear stood singing in harmony with animals in the water, in the air and in the meadow atop the cape. Reggie no longer needed to worry about getting to Windrail in time to vote. He was already there.

Polar Bear on Ice Floe   Reggie Reynard

"No one at the arena was seriously hurt by the blast and Reggie survived his harrowing and unscathed landing in the gulf. But who had won the game?

"The hand on the scratched, dinged and dented game-timing clock pointed to zero. The puck wasn't within the tangled netting of the bent and twisted goal posts, nor was it in Krusher's glove. None of the officials could swear to where it went and despite intensive searches inside the arena, the puck was never found. The final score, unlike the game in Stompin' Tom's *Hockey Song*, was officially ruled to be a tie."

CHAPTER SIXTEEN

CANADA'S BIG FIVE

The Polar Bear on the ice floe at the bottom of Kildare Capes went by the name *Nanuq* (Nanook)," said Grandpa as he carried on with his story. "It means 'the animal worthy of great respect' in the Inuit language. Because they have adopted a marine lifestyle, spend much of their time in the water and take almost all their food from the ocean, polar bears are classified as marine mammals. Their scientific name, *ursus maritimus*, actually means 'Sea Bear.'"

"They're the largest bears in the world and are powerful symbols of strength and endurance in the Canadian Arctic. Canada has honoured them by placing their image on its two dollar coin we call the Twoonie, sometimes spelled 'Toonie.'"

**Twoonie or Toonie
by artist Brent Townsend**

"After Stompin' *Canada Day, Up* thunderous, hair-nearby thicket brought was obvious that a  Tom finished singing his *Canada Way* song, a raising growl from a everyone to attention. It grizzly bear had been appointed Sergeant-at-Arms to maintain order. The two humans immediately excused themselves, leaving the animals alone to deal with the matter of Canada's Big Five.

"Even before Stompin' Tom and Mathilda departed, Nanuq had already been appointed master of ceremonies. The land mammals chose a Canada lynx as their representative, the birds a wise snowy owl. The sea creatures selected one of the smallest of marine mammals, a shy harbour porpoise, to be their leader.

Canada Lynx   Snowy Owl   Harbour Porpoise

"Not much more is known about how the meeting progressed as no minutes were recorded. Apparently the words of wisdom in Nanuq's pre-voting speech had more to do with animal treatment and survival than the popularity of certain breeds. In his address he supposedly said all animals should be provided with as much freedom as possible within their own environment. Allegedly, he also stressed that they should all be treated with equality, dignity and respect regardless of their, type, appearance, status, behaviour, characteristics or perceived importance.

"By early evening when the voting was complete, only the three team leaders and the emcee were aware of the final outcome. The hush-hush would guard against any interference or accusations of meddling. The democratic decision of the animals was placed in a tightly sealed envelope and the outside of the letter was tamper-proofed with a talon-, paw- and fin-print from the three leaders. It was then given to Stompin' Tom for personal delivery to the Prime Minister.

"Stompin' Tom promised the animals he would return to Windrail the following July 1st. If the Prime Minister's reply agreed with them, he would strum, sing, and stomp his *Canada Day, Up Canada Way* song from the very same flat-top

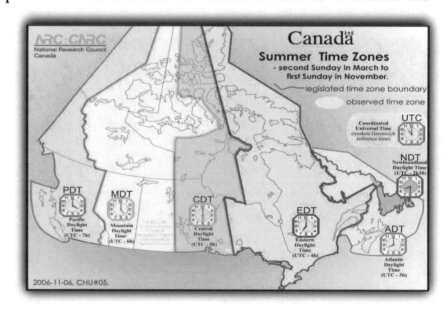

rock. If the majority of Canadians didn't agree with the animals' decision, he would play a different tune.

"By the time the meeting was over, those attending were aware that on the next Canada Day, beginning at noon, Newfoundland Daylight Time (NDT), Stompin' Tom would sing the appropriate song from the flat-topped rock. With the assistance of Noisy Nick, *Wuchowsen*, and the North Cape wind turbines, the song would be repeated from the same location whenever it became twelve o'clock noon in each of the other five time zones. The last would be Pacific Daylight Time covering BC and Yukon."

"How were the animals supposed to tell the time, Grandpa?" asked a concerned Emma.

"I believe your question may be the reason Stompin' Tom chose noon in each zone for his singing times, Emma," answered Grandpa. "Studies show that some animals understand time, but most become aware of it through their five — or maybe even six — senses. At mid-day or noon hour the sun is at its highest, warmest and brightest. Shadows are smaller, food odours are in the air, noon whistles blow, stomachs growl and many humans, being creatures of habit, repeat what they usually do at particular times each day. Those are just some of the many activities, occurrences and changes that can be sensed by animals.

"It isn't a very accurate way to tell time, but fortunately, anxious and enthusiastic early arrivers are usually considerate enough to pass on the information to the tardy," said Grandpa.

"At one time guesstimates, measurements and the noonday sun were the crude methods people around the world had to use to set their clocks and watches. Needless to say, the business hours within and between communities near and far weren't very well coordinated. That is until a Canadian by the name of Sandford Fleming, came up with a better way.

"Fleming was just a teenager when he emigrated to Canada from Scotland to train as a civil engineer. He became the top railway engineer of Canada and, in addition to other railways, was involved in the construction of the CPR. If you look at the photograph of The Last Spike I showed you earlier, he is the tall man in the tallest hat behind the man swinging the spike maul.

"I also showed you an image of Canada's first postage stamp. Its design is the work of the same Sandford Fleming, a man of many talents.

"As train travel grew in popularity and expanded in distance, correct time and coordination became increasingly important. One day Fleming missed his train due to scheduling confusion and decided to do something about it. He divided the world into the number of hours in a day."

"Twenty-four," Traedan burst out.

"Correct," said Grandpa. "It's nice to see you're interested, my boy."

"Fleming divided the world into twenty-four one-hour time zones and presented the system to people around the world. Practically everyone agreed  it was a brilliant idea and adopted it as the world's International Standard Time. It is still in use around the globe today.

Sandford Fleming
Father of Standard Time

168

CHAPTER SEVENTEEN

WAITING FOR THEIR HERO

No one needed to have worried as to whether the animals would be capable of focussing their attention on a future message from Stompin' Tom," began Grandpa, as his small group reassembled after a short leg-stretching session. "One year later, hours before noon, animals all across Canada were impatiently waiting to hear the Prime Minister's ruling on the suggestion they had sent him a year ago. From coast to coast to coast, excitement was building in anticipation of receiving a reply by the promised vibrations. Would they be carried throughout Canada from Stompin' Tom's boot, voice and guitar all the way from the flat-topped rock at Windrail?

"Animals both above and underground felt for the expected tremors by pressing their bodies tightly against the earth. Marine creatures steadfastly fixed their attention on the tickling currents on and below the surface of the ocean, while others closely listened, deep within watery sound channels. With every whisper of wind, the birds did their best to capture some news in airwaves of noise. Everyone was devotedly keeping their sixth sense ability at its keenest edge.

"Elder Mathilda had arrived at Windrail well ahead of the time scheduled for the first broadcast. She hadn't heard from Stompin' Tom in quite some time and hoped he would already be there. She wanted to be sure his guitar and stompin' board were included in her smudging ceremony. Disappointed to find he wasn't present, her concern increased as time went on and he still hadn't made an appearance.

"Although unlikely, she wondered if perhaps Stompin' Tom, like many people have done, had forgotten or become confused by the Newfoundland time zone. Unlike the others, it is only one-half hour ahead of its abutting zone to the west. But that, of course, should have brought Stompin' Tom to Windrail even earlier.

"Stompin' Tom still hadn't shown up when the first performance was due, which would have sent the message to Newfoundland and Labrador. As the clocked ticked closer and closer to noon (ADT) in PEI — the time set for the second message — Windrail was becoming increasingly crowded. Not wishing to miss an opportunity to see and hear their musical hero, many animals from the surrounding area were collecting and clustering atop the cape, in the water below and in the air above.

"Like Murphy's Law - anything that can go wrong will go wrong - even the weather wasn't cooperating. The early morning rays of sunshine that had promised a warm, sunny day began to lose their strength. Light and warmth was no longer penetrating the blanket of damp grey fog rolling in and covering the entire area of *The Secret Meeting Place*. As the temperature continued to drop, a misty spray of rain added to the rising misery and gloom. The dismal weather also increased the feelings of disappointment that had begun to overcome the animals. They wondered and fretted, 'Where is Stompin' Tom?'

"Noisy Nick stood silent and alone nearby, its blades fixed to face and blow north. What it needed was a brisk south wind, not the strong, gusty northerly that had just arrived. Would the wind made by the magical wings of *Wuchowsen* be strong enough to overcome the sudden blasts from the north? Where, oh where, is Stompin' Tom?

"Without Stompin' Tom, there just wasn't anyone at Windrail to send out the sounds and vibrations from the flat-topped rock. Practically hidden in the brown uncut grass, the granite boulder remained eerily quiet and even appeared to have been abandoned by the tiny *Pukulatamuj* spirits once living beneath.

"With time quickly passing, Elder Mathilda tried to contact Stompin' Tom on her cellphone at the number she had used to communicate with him a year ago. The call just added to the mystery when she listened to the recorded reply: 'The number you have dialed is no longer in service.'

"With feelings passing between rejection and worry, the unsettled animals milled about in the woods and meadow. Some glided in slow circles in the sky above the clearing and others breached anxiously out of the sea just to see. Many heads were bowed, some had their tail between their legs, but all appeared forlorn. Why had their trusted icon let them down?

"At that moment, flying out of the hazy dullness, two black birds appeared. Alighting on the still fan blades of Noisy Nick, the two crows caught everyone's attention as they noisily ruffled their feathers and gasped to catch their breath. Recovering quickly from their demanding trip the crows began a loud series of hoarse, grating caws, clicks and coos. It wasn't long before it became apparent they had just flown in all the way from Erin, Ontario, the home of Stompin' Tom.

"Anxiety turned to excitement as the animals grew quiet to listen to the latest news from or about Stompin' Tom. But true to their reputation as messengers of bad news, what the crows had to say wasn't something anyone wanted to  hear. The eyes of the gathered animals, wide open in anticipation of good news, would soon be wet with tears. The crows had come to let them know their Shining Star was now just a memory – Stompin' Tom had passed away.

"Over the hours and for several days thereafter, mournful sounds could be heard whenever news of Stompin' Tom's death reached the ears of animals throughout the nation. From time to time a cougar's high-pitched scream would rip through the air, the sorrowful bugling of an elk, or the haunting howls of coyotes and wolves would echo deep in the forests. From the eerie calls of a loon on a lake, the lonesome sounds of a mourning dove, and the bawling of cattle, to the clicks and whistles of ocean dwellers, animals across Canada became aware of his passing.

"Slowly, word travelled throughout the confused animal world that there would be no timely response to their Big Five decision. In fact, no definite news about Canada's Big Five would ever be received.

Emma asked, "Do you know which animals the animals themselves picked for the Big Five, Grandpa?"

"Apparently none," he told his surprised young descendants. "More significantly, it seems the message from the animals to the Prime Minister only requested that each species remain equal in importance and be properly treated and protected within their own environment to keep them from becoming extinct."

Stompin' Tom's Gravestone, Erin, Ontario Cemetery

CHAPTER EIGHTEEN

THE DISAPPEARING STATUE

In honour of Stompin' Tom," continued Grandpa as he neared the end of his story, "a life-sized statue in his likeness was unveiled in Bell Park, a beautiful municipal park surrounding Lake Ramsay in downtown Greater Sudbury. Even though a couple years had passed, the songs by Canada's favourite troubadour about average people in average towns, were still being played and listened to across his 'Stompin' Grounds.' Played in the chord of A, one of his most famous, *Sudbury Saturday Night*, connected him to that city and its people.

"But animals in and around the Sudbury area seemed unsettled with the statue. On the very first Canada Day after it was erected, an abnormally large number and variety of wildlife seemed to display an unnatural interest in the bronze figure. Many calls were made to the local Fish and Wildlife Conservation Office seeking answers to this rather unusual activity. But by the time a conservation officer arrived at the site to investigate the complaints, all of the animals had disappeared. Except, that is, for a slow-moving porcupine huddled in the branches of a nearby evergreen tree and a wolverine frantically trying to make a quick getaway by digging a hole below the bottom of the fence.

Porcupine

Wolverine

"Unfortunately, and much to the dismay of the responding officer, the sculpture was also missing. He rushed to report the alleged theft to the Greater Sudbury Police. After listening to the details, the Chief of Police assigned his top criminal investigator, Detective Sergeant Wade, to the case.

"When the detective arrived at the scene, he was bewildered and puzzled to find the statue undamaged and back in its proper place as if it had never been tampered with  or removed. Despite his intensive investigative efforts over the next several days, the experienced gumshoe could find no talking eyewitnesses to the event."

"Gumshoe? What's gumshoe?" questioned Traedan, looking down guiltily at the bottom of his slipper to see if he had any bubblegum stuck there.

"It's what they sometimes called detectives a long, long time ago," laughed Grandpa, "because of the soft, gum-rubber-soled shoes they wore back when they did a lot of walking. I guess I'm really showing my age."

"Detective Wade's investigation determined the short period of time between the removal and quick return of the statue, in itself, would have been a humanly impossible task. The returned statue was the original, not a replacement, and there certainly hadn't been enough time known to humanity to alter it in any way. It was returned in perfect condition and displayed no marks of change, damage or discolouration.

"When the crackerjack detective's few leads came to dead ends and all investigative methods were exhausted, there was little more that could be done to explain the mystery. The incident became a Cold Case within the 'Mysterious and Unexplained Files' drawer.

"Before closing and locking the file, Detective Wade slipped in a note of what his trained eagle eye – and no one else – *had* detected.

"Earlier in the investigation, and with his Chief in agreement, the detective had decided to keep the information he discovered confidential. Doing so would prevent the possibility of creating a media frenzy or alarming the public he served.

"The note Detective Wade securely filed away, reads: 'The fingers of Stompin' Tom's left hand are not in the position of an A chord for the song *Sudbury Saturday Night*, but a C chord, probably for the song *Canada Day, Up Canada Way*.'

"The latter was the song Stompin' Tom always played in C and had done so for the animals all across Canada from the flat-topped rock at *The Secret Meeting Place* at Windrail."

Stompin' Tom statue at Bell Park, Sudbury, Ontario
Sculpted by Tyler Fauvelle, Lively, Ontario

"Apparently satisfied, from that day forward, the statue has never again been mobbed by animals. But if you pay close attention to any animal anywhere in Canada at precisely twelve o'clock noon on Canada Day, you will probably notice a difference in their mood as their sixth sense clicks in for the duration of time it would have taken Stompin' Tom to sing his *Canada Day, Up Canada Way* song in the Chord of C.

"The grass in the meadow at *The Secret Meeting Place* has grown tall and Noisy Nick has once again been silenced and hidden by choking vines and sea-mist rust. If, however, you do happen to be at Windrail in Kildare Capes, PEI, and have permission from the owner, take a walk down Old Cellar Lane.

Being careful not to alarm the *Pukulatamuj*, place your palm on the flat-topped rock at precisely noon on July 1ˢᵗ and you just might feel the vibrations. Look up. Listen closely. *Wuchowsen* may be in the air above you.

If a breeze is blowing through the nearby junipers, you may even hear the song *Canada Day, Up Canada Way*. If you do, pick up a flag, wave it high and sing of Canada, strong and free, from sea to sea to sea.

"The Maple Leaf forever...."

"Now it's off to bed," said Grandpa. "Tomorrow will be a busy day with hockey school for both of you first thing in the morning. We'll also be checking on guitar lessons for Traedan and taking a trip to the library to look for the billy goat book for Emma."

ACKNOWLEDGMENTS

Delightful pleasure was what I felt when approval was received from the family and estate of Stompin' Tom Limited supporting my depiction of the late great Canadian singer/songwriter in the storybook manner written. Required permissions were also received through the guidance and generosity of Stompin' Tom Limited manager, Charles Stewart. The efforts of Anthem Entertainment's James Jacoby and Amanda Dworetsky are greatly appreciated as are those of Shari Molstad, music licensing manager at Hal Leonard LLC.

With the approval of Chief Darlene Bernard, information on Mi'kmaq culture and traditions was readily obtained through Sarah Myers, Corinne Dyment and Jamie Thomas of the Lennox Island First Nation community in PEI. An abundance of that knowledge was generously provided by Elder Methilda Knockwood Snache for which I cannot thank her enough.

The internet was an invaluable source of information. Wikipedia displayed public domain and free to copy images. Others came from government institutions, tourist bureau enticements and personal and family collections. A special image came from retired former colleague, OPP Sergeant Ed Linkewich and another from daughter-in-law Christine Bertoli.

I must also mention the cooperation received from the OPP (Commissioner Thomas Carrique), Greater Sudbury Police Service (Chief Paul Pedersen), Toronto Police Service (Chief James Ramer) and Services Board Chair Jim Hart, and the RCMP.

Thanks and acknowledgment also goes out to the following individuals for their initiative, information, support, advice, encouragement, contributions and/or inspiration:

Traedan Karpowich, at the age of two, displayed such courage, bravado and a personality during his battle with cancer it earned him the Ronald McDonald Poster Boy Award; the hockey knowledge of Kelly Karpowich; an education in cell phone speak from a very young Kylie Pasemko; five-year-old American relative, Emma Merritt, living in Florida, USA, with a vast knowledge of Canadiana; the artistic abilities of my grandsons Evan and Rylan; former police tactical unit (OPP TRU) teammate now living in Australia, Terry "Skippy" Drew; my editor (fortunately once again) Kay Griffiths; Alice and Dennis O'Sullivan of the OPP Veterans' Association; Nancy Merriman; Natalie Corcoran; Sharon Baiden; Steven Campoli; Robin Percival; Bella Thrime and her associates at Amazon Publishing Agency; daughter Lesa; son Wade; and, for many years now, my wife and rock, Myra.

Thank you one and all.

ALSO BY ANDREW F. MAKSYMCHUK

COPS: A Matter of Life & Death

From MUSKEG *to* MURDER
Memories of Policing Ontario's Northwest

TRU Tactics and Rescue Unit
The Last Resort in Policing

CHAMPIONS of the DEAD
OPP Crime Fighters Seeking Proof of the Truth

BACK COVER PHOTOS
Author's Private Collection

Top Left:	Skinners Pond Schoolhouse, PEI
Top Right:	Stompin' Tom's traveling truck with his childhood farmhouse foster home in the background. Skinners Pond, PEI
Centre Left:	Highway 12, Kildare Capes, PEI
Centre Right:	Old Cellar Lane to WINDRAIL, Kildare Capes, PEI
Bottom:	Author's pickup truck with OPP plates parked at the Stompin' Tom Centre, Skinners Pond, PEI

Manufactured by Amazon.ca
Bolton, ON

28053154R00103